The Last Real Nigga Alive 3

Tranay Adams

The Last Real Nigga Alive 3

Copyright © 2016 Tranay Adams. All rights reserved.

Warning: The unauthorized reproduction or distribution of this work is illegal. Criminal copyright infringement, including infringement without monetary gain, is investigated by FBI and is punishable by up to five (5) years in federal prison and a fine of $250,000.

All names, characters, and incidents depicted in this book are products of the author's imagination or are used fictitiously. Any resemblance to actual events, locales, organizations, or persons, living or dead, is entirely coincidental, and beyond the intent of the author and publisher.

No part of this book may be reproduced or transmitted in any form or by any means, electronic or mechanical, including photocopying, recording, or by any information storage and retrieval system, without permission in writing from the publisher.

The Last Real Nigga Alive 3 / Tranay Adams-1st ed. © 2016

Kindle Formatting: Renee Lamb

Editor: Ghost

Cover Artist: Sunny Giovanni

Publisher: Tranay Adams

Lafayette's bail had been set and he was bussed to the County jail. Now, he had enough money to post his bail, his only problem was finding someone that he trusted enough to get his stash and bail him out. There wasn't anyone that he could think of that he could count on like that, so he knew he'd be a sitting duck until he could advise some other plan to spring him free from The Belly of the Beast. He was sure that the ballistics had come back on by now, and if they hadn't they would be pretty soon. If that happened, his only way out of his situation would be to escape, and that wouldn't be an easy feat, even with his connections.

Not only did he have the murders on his gun hanging over his head, but the possibility of him getting murdered behind the wall weighed on his shoulders as well. See, as soon as he entered behind the barbed wire walls some Mexican cats were on him like flies on shit. They tried to kill him when he went to go shower but he was able to fend them off. He suffered a few stab wounds but nothing life threatening. Being the G that he was he wanted to go back to general population, but those white folks weren't having that. Nah, they put his black ass in involuntary protective custody.

Lafayette had a lot of alone time, so he kept himself busy with his contraband cell phone. If he wasn't jacking off to porn then he was watching movies. One night after making an important call, he lay back in his bunk with his hands steepled behind his head. He found his eyelids growing heavier and heavier with each minute that passed by until they eventually shut. The nigga was asleep when the door of his cell was unlocked and a correctional officer stepped inside.

***

Lafayette's eyes fluttered open. His vision was blurry, but it came back into focus after a while. He gave himself the once over, seeing that he was bound to a chair by heavy silver chains. Although he was restrained, it didn't stop him from trying to get loose. His struggling caused the chair that he was perched in to slide slightly across the floor. He attempted this for a while and all it did was tire him, leaving him breathing hard. His chest inflated and deflated, as he inhaled and exhaled, looking about. He was inside of the shower room, which was dimly lit. He looked around for someone or something that would lead him to his salvation, but there wasn't anyone or anything in sight. A moment later, he heard footsteps come from his left. When he looked a correctional officer came to a stop inside of the doorway, standing off to the side. He looked in at the mothafucka bound to the chair and then folded his arms across his chest, leaning up against the doorway. Soon after there was whistling, drawing closer and closer. Then there was the sound of something metal being drug on the cement floor. The noise stopped at the door way. There was the silhouette of a short man carrying something long and curved at its end. He patted the C.O on the arm and stepped inside of the shower room, walking in Lafayette's direction. The closer he got to the hustler, the more he began to fill out under the dim lighting that the shower room provided. The short man suddenly stopped before Lafayette. His face was partially hidden by the darkness of the room so the hustler peered closer to identify him. When recognition ripped through his brain, he had to blink a few times to be sure of who was standing before him.

"Lil…Lil…Lil…" he stammered.

"Lil Man, alive and in the mothafucking flesh," The little nigga smiled wickedly and tapped the pipe in his palm.

Lafayette was speechless, he couldn't believe it. A walking, talking, dead man stood right before his eyes.

"They had me caged up in P.C, after that amateur ass hit them pussies laid down." Lil Man put it out there. "Them folks put the word out that I was dead for my protection, them other niggaz never seen it coming when I put in the order to have'em hit." Homie bound to the chair eyes doubled in size and his mouth formed an O, seeing the little nigga tapping the pipe into his palm. "You betrayed me; I would have rotted inside this shithole for you! It crushed me when I found out that it was you that put the green light on me! Disloyalty is a violation punishable by death! And your sentencing has come, Lafayette!" He brought the pipe above his head and brought it down with all of his might.

Cling! Crack!

Lafayette's chin slammed into his chest and the top of his skull cracked open like a mothafucking egg. His brain and blood bubbled out the top of his scalp, oozing down over his face. Lafayette's fingers and legs twitched, his tongue hung out of his mouth. Again, Lil Man brought the pipe down with all of his might, speckling his jumpsuit with blood. Again, again, and again, he struck down upon his enemy with hatred and furious anger. The powerful blows cracked Lafayette's skull open further and further, sending brain fragments sliding down his face and dropping wet into his lap. Lil Man brought his pipe down and allowed it to dangle at his side. He stared down at the mess he had created, chest rising and falling rapidly, mouth open as he took husky breaths. He spat off to the side and tossed the pipe aside.

"Rest in shit," Lil' Man's eyes lingered on his victim for a time. He was about to turn to walk away, when something caught his eyes. "What the fuck?" he uttered in disbelief.

***

Jason sat on the living room couch twisting his platinum wedding band around his finger. It was 3 o'clock in the morning and Montrice hadn't made it home yet. His gut told him that she was more than likely out fucking around, which made him wish he wouldn't have canceled the contract he'd put out on her. For as heated as he was he couldn't bring himself to go along with having her murdered. He hated to admit it to himself but he had a conscience. And if he allowed himself to be involved with her demise it would haunt him for the rest of his life. He didn't need that shit, so he decided that it was best that they get a divorce.

Jason pulled off his wedding ring and placed it on the nightstand. Afterwards, he picked up the cordless telephone to place a call to Montrice. That's when he heard the door bell chime downstairs. He sat the cordless phone back on the nightstand and went down the staircase. He glanced through the peephole and saw two detectives on his front porch. His forehead wrinkled wondering what the two men were doing at his house at this hour. Thinking nothing of it, he unchained, unlocked and snatched the door open.

"Are you Jason Shakur?" The Latin Detective asked. He nodded yes. "Sorry to disturb you at this hour, Mr. Shakur. I'm Detective Francisco Rivera and this is my partner Detective Dawayne Bishop." He flashed his badge before sticking it back inside of his overcoat. "We're here about your wife, Officer Montrice Shakur."

"Is she OK?" Jason adjusted his glasses, looking between the two detectives.

Detective Rivera took a deep breath and exhaled. "You mind if we come inside for a moment?"

Jason opened the door wider and stepped aside; leaving a clear path for the two detectives to enter. The detectives came inside of the Shakur residence and sat down on the couch. Jason shut and locked the door behind him. He made his way over to them and asked could he get them a cup of coffee, which they declined.

"We regret to inform you that your wife was murdered." Bishop informed him.

"Mur...murdered?" Jason's eyes grew big and his mouth dropped open. He stumbled backwards and plopped down on the sofa. His world was spinning out of control, he couldn't believe it. How could she be dead when he took the check off of her head? Surely the nigga that he had hired didn't pull the trigger. They'd agreed that he could keep the bag, just as long as he didn't go through with her execution.

"Yes. Murdered," Bishop repeated.

"Look, Mr. Shakur, your wife didn't have any beefs, did she?" Rivera asked him. "Was there anyone that may have wanted to see her dead?" Jason leaned forward and brought his hand down his face, taking a deep breath. "Mr. Shakur, did you hear me?"

The police didn't have any clue of Montrice being on that block to plant kilos of cocaine in Lafayette's car. Before the law had gotten there a couple of crackheads had snatched the duffle bag of drugs that she was carrying. As far as the police knew, little momma was in the hood visiting someone or some shit.

Jason looked up at the detectives and said, "No. I'm sorry."

"Did your wife have any beefs that we need to know about?"

"Are you kidding me, detective? My wife was a cop. There's no telling how many assholes out there had a vendetta against her."

The detectives exchanged glances.

"He's got a point." Rivera told his partner. Bishop nodded his agreement.

"Jesus H. Christ, tell me this is a nightmare, detectives." Jason slumped in the chair and shut his eyelids, massaging the bridge of his nose.

Rivera reached inside of his overcoat and pulled out his card, holding it out to Jason. "I wish I could, I really do. Here, give me a call should anything come to mind that may help us in solving her murder."

Jason sat up and took the card from him, looking it over. "Sure thing."

The detectives shook hands with Jason and they took their leave. Once they were gone, he grabbed his keys and ran out of the house. He jumped into his Mercedes Benz CLK and backed out of the driveway. Swinging out into the street, he floored the gas pedal and took off down the block.

***

"Follow me," the pathologist motioned for Jason to follow him as he made his way down the hallway, chewing bubble gum. He was a tall, white man with a balding scalp and big ass glasses. He had a nose as large as a buzzard's beak and thin, pink lips. The lab coat he wore fit him like a trench coat; it swayed from left to right, as he made his way down the corridor.

The pathologist crossed the threshold inside of the morgue, flipping on the light switch. As soon as he activated it, the overhead lights cut on one by one, illuminating the large room. Jason came in right behind the pathologist, the first thing he smelled was death and what he believed was some kind of cleaning solution lingering in the air. The scent was overwhelming, but he tried to ignore it as best as he could. Jason looked from left to right, taking in his surroundings. There were sinks and tables on the left and a couple of small rooms on the right. There was also a gallery on the right with windows. Ahead of him there were about seventeen dead naked mothafuckaz lying on gurneys underneath white sheets. Their feet were sticking out of the bottom of the sheets and there was a tag on their big toe.

A whistle drew Jason's attention to the far corner of the room. When he looked he found the pathologist standing behind one of the dead bodies that was underneath a sheet. He blew an enormous pink bubble and it popped. Afterwards, he motioned him over and he come speed walking over. He came to stand on the opposite side of the gurney that the body was laying on, looking down. The pathologist asked if he was ready to see underneath the sheet and he nodded yes. Without further due, he threw the sheet from over the upper half of the body. Jason's eyes instantly misted when he saw Montrice laid on the gurney before him. Seeing the devastation on the attorney's face, he took a deep breath and chewed on his gum.

"Is this your wife?" he asked Jason and he nodded, wiping the tears that trickled. "I'll give you a minute." He patted him on the shoulder and went on about his business, leaving the man to his wife.

"Why did you leave me, sweetheart? I love you so much," Jason said, dripping teardrops onto her face that splashed against her cheeks. Sneakily, he glanced over his shoulder and saw the pathologist on the other side of the room, writing something down on a clipboard. He turned his attention back around to Montrice's corpse. His eyebrows dipped low and a shit-eating-grin broadened his face. "Fucking cunt, you got the nerve to cheat on me and let the next nigga knock you up? I should have never married you; my mother told me you weren't worth a goddamn." He hawked up phlegm and spit on her face. He watched as the nasty goo slid down the shape of her nose. Hearing someone approaching at his rear, he looked over his shoulder and saw the pathologist approaching, blowing a bubble with his gum. Quickly, he turned back around and wiped his saliva off of her face with the sleeve of his shirt. Right then he went back to his fake grieving, shoulders shuddering and eyes oozing tears. The pathologist came up behind him and gripped his shoulder, giving him some emotional support.

"That's it, let it out, let it all out." He told him and swept the sheet back over Montrice's corpse. The pathologist chopped it up with Jason a time longer about him and his wife's history. Afterwards, the attorney made his way towards the door, wiping and blowing his nose with a Kleenex. "Poor bastard all broken up about his wife," He looked on with his hands on his hip, blowing a large bubble until it exploded.

***

The Mercedes came to a screeching halt and Jason hopped out. He slammed his door shut and made his way across the street, looking both ways as he went along. Fishing inside of his pocket, he pulled out a fist of change and counted out the coins he'd need to make a call. He crossed paths with a homeless man pushing a shopping cart with garbage bags of cans and bottles attached to it. He also clipped shoulders with a pedestrian who was listening to his headphones and nodding his head. Homie caught an attitude. He scowled and looked like he was about to fire on him but Jason apologized. Seeing that Jason didn't want any static, the pedestrian called him a 'punk ass nigga' and pulled the headphones back over his ears. He went about his business, nodding his head to the music and reciting the lyrics.

Jason made it to one of the only working payphones by his house. He snatched up the receiver and rubbed it off on his shirt. Reaching inside of his jeans, he pulled out a wrinkled, folded piece of paper. After dropping the coins into the slot of the payphone, he unfolded the piece of paper. Looking back and forth between the piece of paper and the numbered buttons on the payphone, he punched the telephone number in. Switching the telephone to his other ear and cradling it with his shoulder, he listened to the line ring. Occasionally, he looked over his shoulder to see if anyone was watching him. They weren't.

We're sorry, but the number you have reached is no longer in service.

Jason frowned up hearing this automated recording. He hung the telephone up and looked the digits on the piece of paper over again. He was sure that he had dialed these very numbers, but to be sure he was going to try it again. Picking the telephone back up, he dropped the coins into the slot and dialed the number up again. Again, he got the same recording. Defeated, he hung the telephone up and balled up the piece of paper, letting it drop to the sidewalk. Shoving his hands into his pockets, he strolled off into the night wondering exactly who it was that whacked out his wife.

Chapter One

Loon stepped to the commode and unzipped his jeans, pulling out his meat. He parted his legs and tilted his head back. A relieved expression came across his face as he pissed into the toilet bowl. Once he was done, he gave his limp dick to shakes before putting it back inside of its denim prison and zipping back up. Flushing, he walked to the porcelain sink and turned on the water. Lathering his hands, he held them under the flowing water, occasionally glancing at his appearance in the medicine cabinet mirror. His eyebrows arched and his nose crinkled, seeing all of the damage that had been done to him due to Gar beating him with his gun.

Loon's face was twice its size and his left eye was swollen shut. He had black and blue bruising underneath both eyes and six cuts on his face. His leg was also in a cast having been shot twice. Seeing himself in his current state made him mad as a mothafucka. He had business in the streets that he needed to attend to, but, fuck that; it could take the backseat to him getting his revenge. He didn't know where that nigga Gar was laid up, but he knew one thing, he was going to find his ass and kill him.

Crack!

He slammed his fist into the mirror and it cracked into a spider's cobweb. When he drew his fist back it had small cuts on it from the assault. He looked down into the sink and saw pieces of broken glass that twinkled like diamonds, sprinkled with dots of blood. Loon snatched a washcloth from off of the rack where it was laying on a towel. He wrapped the washcloth around his fist and used his teeth to tie it up. Afterwards, he left the bathroom and entered his master bedroom, opening the closet door. He pulled the drawstring and the light bulb inside of the closet gave the space light. Parting his clothes that were hanging on the rack, he exposed the AK-47 lying up against the wall. He snatched the deadly weapon up and checked the banana clip, that bitch was fully loaded so he smacked it back in. Holding the assault rifle down at his side in one hand, he limped out of the closet and entered the hallway. Pulling out his cellular, he called up the nigga he had business with that night.

"'Sup, my nigga? Nah, homie, I'ma have to get up witchu later on, some shit came up. Cool." He hung up and stuck the cell phone into his pocket. When came out the backdoor, he headed over to his old school Buick Regal and slid in behind the wheel, cranking that thang up. The headlights came on and smoke wafted from the exhaust pipes. Putting the vehicle into drive, he pulled off and drove down his driveway. He cruised through the streets wearing a scowl, the street lights flashing on and off of his face. He took the time to fire up a half smoked blunt that was lying inside of the ashtray. After he sucked on the end of it, he blew out a big cloud of smoke.

Loon didn't know exactly where to find Gar, but he did remember the tattoo on his neck from the night he'd beat him in his face with his Tec-9. The ink was in honor of his hood, The Eastside Rolling 20s Bloods. Loon knew exactly where that hood was. It was on the lower eastside in a section notoriously known as The Low Bottoms. He may not know what street that he stayed on, but he was sure he'd figure out a way to find his whereabouts. As quickly as the idea came to Loon's mind, he was hopping on the 110 freeway heading east to that nigga Gar's hood.

***

Gar lay in his hospital bed in darkness, eyelids shut, mouth forming a straight line. The only thing that could be heard was the noises that the medical machinery made, as they worked to keep him alive. Suddenly, his eyelids and his fingers twitched. He was reliving the night that he was shot. It was a night that he'd never forget. He'd just come back from trying to blow that nigga Loon's head off. Unfortunately, he wasn't able to knock his ass off because his Tec-9 had jammed up on him.

Pissed off, he beat the mothafucka in the face with it and sped off in his whip. Afterwards, he went to the trap house to check on things.

Flashback

Gar hopped out of the rental and made his way into the front-yard of the trap. His forehead wrinkled when he noticed that the lights were off. He glanced at the screen of his cell phone and wondered what the lights were doing off at that hour. The trap was normally jumping at that hour with activity. He found it strange that it was as dead as a limp dick.

Gar walked upon the porch and knocked on the front-door. He waited a while but no one answered. He tried to peek inside of the window, but the curtains were blocking his view. That's when he decided to walk around to the side of the house to try the side door. Once he was there he twisted the knob, and surprisingly the door opened. Once he'd stepped inside of the house, he flipped on the light switch but the lights didn't come on. He flipped the light switch on and off rapidly, but the lights still didn't come on. Gar dipped into the pocket of his Levi's and pulled out a Bic lighter. His thumb brushed down hard on the metal mechanism of the lighter and a flame was conceived, licking the air.

Gar made his way through the darkness with his lighter leading the way, its golden orange illumination shone on his face. When he came across something in the corner of the kitchen, he turned around. His forehead wrinkled when he saw Naughty sitting in the corner in a chair with his throat slit from ear to ear. A light shined on Gar's face from his right, blinding him. He whipped around and Auntie was holding a flashlight in his face with a gun extended underneath it. When Gar saw the handgun he dropped his lighter and broke for the side door, sneakers screeching on the linoleum floor.

Boc! Boc! Boc!

The first bullet slammed into Gar causing him to howl in pain. A second one slammed into his shoulder as he made it to the doorway of the side door, dripping blood along the way. The third one splintered the wood of the doorway and sprayed debris everywhere. Gar had made it out of the door and was staggering down the walkway as fast as he could, holding his bleeding shoulder, blood oozed from between his fingers. He'd just made it to the front of the house when Diana appeared out of nowhere. Mad dogging him, she lifted her banger and squeezed the trigger. A bullet slammed into Gar's lower abdomen and doubled him over wincing. He staggered backwards. He tried to grab a hold of something to stop from falling, but ended up grabbing air. Gar fell to the ground on his back, staring up at the sky and breathing heavily. Auntie emerged from the doorway of the side door, clutching her banger in one hand and a flashlight in the other. She moved in to finish her victim off, leveling her banger between his eyes. Diana walked over and stood beside her, pointing her banger at Gar as well. Lying on his back, all he could see were the silhouettes of the women and the hollowed faces of their weapons.

Damn, I guess this is it, Gar thought, I can't be mad though. I'm gone get it how I lived it. When it's all said and done, they're gonna bury me a G.

Bloc!

Gar lay on the ground watching his homeboy Lafayette finish off Auntie and Diana. Before he knew it darkness had claimed.

Present

Gar's eyelids and lips peeled open to slits. His face balled up and wrinkles formed at the corners of his eyes. He was still in pain, feeling the wounds he'd suffered by the hands of the vengeful crackheads. Homeboy was angry at himself for being caught slipping. There wasn't any way in hell that those old bitches should have gotten so close to killing him. If he would have taken a dirt nap he was sure a G of his caliber would have been the laughing stock in Heaven or Hell, whichever he was going to once he kicked the bucket.

Gar's toes wiggled and his fingers moved animatedly, appearing as if they were coming back to life. The green line of the heart monitor moved in a zig zag pattern across the black screen. The heart monitor and the rest of the medical machinery were the only noises inside of the hospital room.

Niggaz had him fucked up if they thought that he was going to lie down and die. Fuck that, before he shut his eyelids forever, he was going to take some of his enemies with him.

***

The night was quiet except for the conversing between two hood niggaz. They stood on the block passing a smoldering blunt between them, casually blowing out clouds of smoke. One was wearing a red Chicago Bulls beanie and matching jersey. His eyes were hooded from the weed he'd consumed. He was rather tall, possessing a long face and a scrawny body. This was T.K. His homie standing beside him was a lot chunkier, wearing a red and black checkered shirt that was buttoned at the top and cornrows. This was Fat Daddy. It was obvious that the two were gang affiliated. They more than likely belonged to the 20s Bloods, which was right up Loon's alley, because he was looking for one of them niggaz to squeeze some information out of.

Unbeknownst for the hood niggaz they weren't alone. They were being watched like they were under surveillance by the F.B.I. The niggaz were so high that they were ignorant to the presence of immense danger, but sure enough it was right there, observing them from the darkness, just far enough to hear their conversation.

"Yo' where did you get this shit from?" T.K asked Fat Daddy, smoke wafting around him.

"That fool Hector. My ese homie, you met 'em at that lil' kick back on the Westside, rememba, Fat Daddy?"

"Oooooh yeahhh, I rememba, Blood, he's cool people. Where you know that fool from, T.K?"

The conversation went on as Loon coasted up on him, turning down his music. Caught off guard, T.K and Fat Daddy stiffened up like a pair of dicks.

"'Sup, Blood? Y'all seen that nigga Gar?" Loon inquired, looking between them.

"Fuck is you, homeboy?" Fat Daddy brandished something silver and shiny. It gleamed under the dim street lights. Loon caught him pulling it but he wasn't worried. From the looks of it, he gathered it was a nickel plated .22.

"Blood, it's me."

"Fuck is me, nigga?" Fat Daddy said, looking closer. He was a second away from popping Loon's ass.

"On the set, Fat Daddy, you on some funny shit, I just finished talking to you."

"Hen Dog?" his forehead wrinkled with confusion.

"Yeah, Blood, it's me."

"Ooooh, my bad, homie," He tucked his gun on his waist-line. A look of relief came over him and T.K's face. "Blood, you almost got the business out here creeping up and shit. What up, fool?"

"That nigga Gar, man, I needa holla at 'em."

Fat Daddy and T.K exchanged glances.

"Bro, you ain't heard? That nigga Gar got popped by them smoker bitches, Auntie and Diana." T.K finally spoke up.

Loon's face balled up and wrinkles formed across the beginning of his nose. "He's dead?"

"Naw, he ain't dead, that fool laid up at the 'spital."

"Which one?"

"County General.

"Oh yeah? What name is he under?"

"His government…Clarence Spivey."

Fat Daddy said, brows furrowing. "Yo' for real. I could have sworn I told you what happened to blood already."

T.K looked back at his chunky homeboy and said, "I could have sworn that too, ol' forgetful ass nigga. Blood smoke to much weed." They laughed and dapped each other up.

"Fuck y'all niggaz, man," Loon busted up laughing, showing all thirty-two teeth inside of his mouth. As fast as you can snap your fingers, his eyebrows arched and his nose scrunched up. He snarled and pointed his AK-47 out of the window, Fat Daddy and T.K's eyes bulged.

Blatatatatatatatat!

T.K took all that heat to his chest and fell back, arms flailing up in the air. His eyelids were squeezed shut and his mouth was stretched wide open, revealing all of the cavities in his mouth. Fat Daddy grabbed his .22, but before he could clear it from his waistline, he was getting chopped down.

Blatatatatatatatat!

His big ass dropped on his behind, head bowed and palms facing up. The front of his shirt was soaked in blood. Loon pulled his choppa back inside of the Buick Regal and coasted by, taking the time to observe his handiwork. Satisfied with the hood niggaz deaths, he drove off and whipped out his cell phone. He made a call. The line ringed three times before someone finally picked up.

"Yo' C-Bo, I need you to gather up the homies…"

***

"You're finished, pal, washed up." The D.E.A agent told Zay as he handcuffed his wrists behind his back. The muscle bound bandit wasn't paying him any mind though. Nah, he was focused on his crying wife, who was also being hand-cuffed. As the agent went on talking shit about Zay and his wife were never going to see the light of day again, homie kept right on speaking to his lady.

"I love you, La' Chat." He said, looking her straight in her eyes and grinning.

"I love you too, bae. You're the man of my dreams and my reality." This was the last thing that she said to him before she was placed into the backseat of an unmarked car, door slamming shut on her. She quickly scooted to the window of the vehicle and looked out at her man; he'd just been placed in the back of an unmarked car as well. They stared out at one another as their respective vehicles were started up. The cars pulled off, with the couples communicating through the windows. They'd use their hot breaths to fog up the glass and their noses to write a message in it.

I have no regrets, I'd live this life with you all over again, La' Chat wrote on the fogged up window.

So would I, Zay wrote back to her in his fogged up window.

Once the white smear from his breath disappeared from off of the window, he fogged it up again. He then wrote his name and her name, with the infinity symbol at the center of them. When she seen this she broke down sobbing. She then sniffled and fought back her tears, writing back to him, Forever. He nodded to her, letting her know that's what he meant, her and him forever.

Zay let his forehead fall against the window and submitted to his emotions, breaking down crying. His shoulders shudder and tears flooded his cheeks, he turned his face away from the window so his wife wouldn't see him in this state. She reacted the same way that he did, turning her face away from the window. At that moment the respective unmarked cars departed from one another, one trailing after the other.

Zay and La'Chat drifted off to sleep crying. When they finally awoke, they'd be ready to face the consequences for their actions.

Chapter Two

Loon pulled up across the street from the hospital and murdered the engine. He grabbed the AK-47 from off of the backseat and he racked that bitch, making sure it was locked and loaded. While he was doing this, he took an involuntary glance at himself in the rearview mirror and his face balled up. His glassy eyes took on a menacing appearance and wrinkles formed across the beginning of his nose. All of the bruises and cuts littering his face made him angry all over again. His blood began boiling and he felt hotness around his ears and the back of his neck. He balled his gloved hand into a fist and it shook slightly. Suddenly, his hand snapped open and he touched his injuries.

Oh, yeah, this bitch ass nigga getting the whole kay clip, on me, Loon thought to himself. He then popped open the glove-box and pulled out a ski-mask. He held it in both of his hands and stared down at it. Every time he put this mothafucka on a nigga or some niggaz lost their lives. He was an entirely different person once he pulled that mask over his face. He wasn't Loon, he wasn't Tanerio McGowan. Nah, he wasn't any of those niggaz. He was a straight up, cold blooded killa, for real.

As soon as Loon pulled the ski-mask over his face and took a look in the rearview mirror to adjust the eye holes in it, a big ass charcoal gray Excursion pulled to a squealing halt outside of his door. This startled him, and he went to point his assault rifle at whoever was in the driver seat. He fell back once he saw his niggaz C-Bo and Tombstone in the front seat. Them niggaz were dressed in beanies and wearing all black, hardcore expressions written across their faces. Loon had hit them up on his way over to the location. He was about to lay a hit down and he needed some back up. The nigga was going on a suicide mission, but he didn't give a fuck. His reputation, his pride, and his ego were on the line and he had to do something about it. Fuck that!

"Y'all fools almost got the business pulling up like that?" Loon spat heatedly at his goons.

"Man, fuck all of that," Tombstone waved him off like he didn't want to hear that shit right now. "Who are these niggaz that needa get they shit split?"

"You mean *the nigga,* and he's the one that did this?" Loon pointed to the damage that had been done to his face. "It's the same mothafucka that beat me in the face with a Tec-9, and his ass is up there in that 'spital." He pointed across the street to the hospital and his goons' heads snapped to it. "Y'all niggaz know the deal, mask up so we can go do this shit."

Tombstone and C-Bo looked at that nigga like he had lost his mothafucking mind.

"My nigga, have you lost yo' goddamn mind?" C-Bo asked. "I just got outta the mothafucking pen on my second strike. You talking 'bout running up in the hospital blazing? Where I know The Ones are gonna be crawling like roaches? Hell naw, fuck that. You my nigga, and I love you to death, but I can't go out like that, homie!"

"I can't believe this shit, man, you bitching up?" Loon balled his face tighter.

"He's gotta point, its badges all up and through that bitch. We'd have to be some crazy mothafuckaz to run up in there shooting."

"You two niggaz should have showed up in thongs and skirts and left the choppas at home," He shook his head pitifully and massaged the bridge of his nose.

"Yo, what the fuck niggaz gone do?" Cuba leaned into the front seat. He and this other young nigga Biggie were in the backseat. They were younger than the collective, but they were just as dangerous. "Niggaz is out in the middle of…" he stopped himself short when a Buick Regal drove past them. He then focused his attention back on the conversation at hand. "Niggaz is out in the middle of the streets with them thangs and it ain't no telling when the opps gone slide through."

"That's what I'm talking about, either we gone do it or we not." Biggie finally spoke up.

"That's what I'm saying," Loon said, then turned to C-Bo and Tombstone, "So, y'all niggaz with this shit or what?"

C-Bo shook his head and stood his ground, "Nah. It's like I told you before, I'm not going out like that."

Tombstone took a deep breath, looking from his homie behind the wheel to Loon. From the expression on his face they both could tell that he was mulling things over in his head before he gave him his final decision. "I'm good, my nigga, I'm falling back on this one."

With the answers given, Loon pulled his mask from off of his face and looked to his niggaz in the SUV, "Yo, man, y'all niggaz pull over to the side of the road."

"For what?" C-Bo frowned.

"Nigga, just pull the fuck over," He directed with his finger. C-Bo took a deep breath and pulled over to the curb where that nigga Loon had directed him. Loon watched from behind the wheel through his windshield as the truck pulled over, smoke wafting from out of its chrome exhaust pipes. Homeboy slid out of his ride, slamming the door shut behind him and leaving his assault rifle behind. He spat off to the side and limped up on the driver side of the Excursion, hands behind his back.

"'Sup, nigga?" C-Bo looked out of the driver side window as Loon came to a stop before him. He scowled and lifted up a .32 with two hands, a silencer at the end of its barrel. He squeezed off the small gun with rapidly succession, flames spitting.

Choot! Choot!

C-Bo and Tombstone's dome exploded. Pieces of their skulls and brain fragments splattered on the dashboard and the leather seats.

"Hoe ass niggaz out here scared to ride." Loon hustled over to the driver side door and opened it. As he let the windows up he hollered at the young niggaz in the backseat. "Y'all niggaz still riding out or what?" he asked the young killas, who looked like they were shocked that he'd popped off so suddenly. It tripped them the fuck out because everybody in the truck was like family. It was at that moment that they realized that, that family shit went out of the window when the rest of the homies weren't trying to ride.

"Yeah, we still riding." Biggie said.

"Cool. Y'all niggaz hop out and go get in my car." With that said, the young killas jumped out of the SUV, slamming their doors shut. AK-47s held at their sides, they darted over to Loon's ride, heads on a swivel for the cops or any possible witnesses. The threesome boarded the vehicle and parked at the back of the hospital, where they were sure no one would spot them invading the facility.

***

Bump! Bump! Bump! Bump!

Victoria banged the back of her head as she was drug down the basement's staircase by her hair kicking and screaming. On the third bump her eyes rolled to the back of her head and she moaned, barely conscious. With that, she lay completely still as she was drug across the floor by Diablo. The drug lord's henchmen stood in the background with their choppas. They watched as their boss shackled the queen pin's ankle and neck. Afterwards, he stepped to the front of her, staring her dead in her mothafucking eyes. Suddenly, she hawked up phlegm and spat it into his face. He squeezed his eyelids shut as the nasty goo slid down his face, outlining the shape of his nose. She threw her head back laughing harder and harder. Slowly, he pulled a rag from out of the back of his pocket and wiped it off of his face. Next, he smiled wickedly and folded the rag up, sliding it into his back pocket. The queen pin was still laughing hardily, so he decided to shut her ass up.

Bwap!

A gut punch knocked the wind out of her, causing her eyes to bulge and her jaw to drop wide open. Then came another, and another, then another. Her eyes bulged more and more, and then she threw up her dinner from that night. The goop was pinkish green with chunks of unidentifiable food in it. It splattered against the floor, and some of it even got on the tip of her shoe.

Victoria and her men hit Diablo's mansion with full force. They took out the few men that he had guarding his estate and closed him on him. He fled towards the back of the house, bullets flying back and forth across his body. Occasionally, he'd stop and take a shot at his pursuers, killing a couple of the men in the process. He found him running towards his enormous garage. Opening the door, he ran inside, but a grenade came rolling in behind him. Seeing it at his feet, he took off running. He'd almost cleared the area of the blast when the grenade exploded, sending him hollering and flying across the air. His arm hit the roof of a Mercedes van and it fractured. He landed on his side wincing and holding his arm. Lying on the floor, he saw several booted feet flooding the garage and his eyes lit up.

He knew that he had to get the fuck out of there before it was too late. Quietly, he opened the driver side door of a

BMW 745 and popped its trunk. Having shut the door gently, he crawled to the rear of the vehicle and climbed into the back of it, shutting it behind him. Lying in the trunk, he listened to Victoria's men shooting up his cars and then checking them. Shutting his eyelids, he mouthed a prayer and rubbed the tattoo of the Virgin Mary on his hairy chest. As he was doing this, bullets were puncturing holes through the vehicle that he was in the trunk of. Some of the rounds went through the trunk and small rays of light shined in through the holes. Luckily for Diablo he went unscathed. Giving up on the search for him, Victoria's men set fire to all of the vehicles inside of the garage before taking their leave. Diablo heard some of the cars exploding, while he was growing hot himself inside of the trunk. He knew he had to get out fast, so he shot holes through the backseat's fabric and tore it open. He oozed through the opening, unlocked the car and hopped out. Looking around he saw several of his burning automobiles. When he looked to the small door of the gas tank it was burning and the paint was bubbling and tearing. He took off running out of the garage. He'd just cleared the threshold when the finale explosion sent his flying high into the air. It came splashing down inside of his pool. When he swam back up to the surface, he took in the full scope of his estate, everything was a burning inferno.

Diablo was the head honcho of his empire so he didn't have to get his hands dirty. He had killas for all of that shit. He would have let them handle it, but mothafuckaz had knocked off his brother and sister. With them getting at his family like that, he had to jump out there in the field and let blood answer for blood. He couldn't just let his hired hands do the shit, because he wouldn't be able to sleep at night knowing that he wasn't the one that had put in the work.

After the attack on his mansion Diablo banded his most fierce men and took a trip across the border to seek his revenge. He kidnapped Victoria with plans of torturing and killing her, which would satisfy his thirst for vengeance.

"That was the setup, now here's the punch-line!" Diablo cracked her in the face with his casted arm, fracturing her nose. Once again her eyes rolled into the back of her head, flashing white. A crimson ring appeared on her nose and her head bobbled about. He stood there breathing hard, chest expanding and shrinking. He grabbed her by the lower half of her face so hard that her lips puckered up, blood sliding down between his thumb and index finger. Having studied her face, he shoved his tongue inside of her mouth and French kissed her, deep and hard. Right after, he was unbuckling his belt and unzipping his tight ass jeans. He pulled out his semi-erect dick and spat into his palm. His henchmen looked on as he used his saliva to lube up his member until it was bone hard. Shoving his boxers and jeans down around his thighs, he tore the clothing from off of her, like they were the plastic wrapping from off of a brand new CD. Grabbing her by the back of her neck aggressively, he took a firm hold of himself and drove it up her pussy violently. The pain sent shock waves throughout her body and her eyelids snapped open. She was choked up taking his grown man up her vagina, feeling her womanhood tear. She rocked back and forth during the entire violation, the chains of the shackles making noises.

"Uh! Uh! Uh! Uh!" Diablo rammed himself up inside of her, blood oozing around his manhood. His hands were planted on her shoulders and he was working up quite the sweat. His eyelids were narrowed into slits and his jaws were locked. He wasn't trying to fuck her. Nah, he was trying to destroy her from the inside out. "You wanna play with the big boys, huh? Well, welcome to the fucking league! Uh! Uh! Uh! Uh! Fucking whore! Fucking cunt!"

"Ahhhhhhhh!" she threw her head back and shrilled at the top of her lungs, shaking her head back and forth. He continued to punish her from behind, without any remorse.

"That's right, bitch, take this mothafucking dick! Uh! Uh! Uh! Uh!" he went harder and harder, pummeling from her rear, his pelvis slapping up against her buttocks.

"Fuck you! Fuck you! Fuck you! Rahhhhhh!" she looked back at him watching him violate her. She mad dogged him and gritted, showing him that she could take whatever he threw at her. "Is that all you got? Huh? Huh? You fucking spic!" Hearing her taunting him, Diablo went that much harder and dropping more sweat. "Hahahahahahahahaha!"

"You fucking whore! Shut up! Shut up!" he grew angrier and pounded her harder and faster, rasping out of breath.

"Hahahahahahahahaha!" her eyes lit up and she laughed even harder at his ass. She had to show that mothafucka that he couldn't break her no matter what he did to her. She had to show him that she was one of the baddest bitches to have ever been pushed out of a woman's womb. "Raaaaaahhhhhh!" she roared and gritted, still looking back at him. She continued to rock back and forth from him raping her, but he had begun to slow down. He was exhausted and on top of that his dick had gone limp.

"Fuck!" he shouted and spat more profanities in Spanish. He pulled out of her and looked down at his limp bloody dick. He grabbed it and tried stroking it back to life, but that bitch was dead as a doorknob. He cussed under his breath and tugged it feverishly.

"Hahahahahahahahahaha," Victoria laughed manically. "Weak ass, bitch ass, wet-back ass nigga, you can't get it up? Huh?"

"Shut up! Shut the fuck up!" Diablo shouted, spittle flying from out of his mouth. He pulled his jeans up with one hand and used the other to crack her ass in the back of the skull. Upon impact she crashed to the floor barely conscious. Staring down at her, he zipped up his jeans and buckled his belt. "You think shit is funny, huh? Well, I hope you get a kick outta this." He then addressed all eight of his henchmen. "You guys want some pussy?" they all said yes. "She's all yours." He grabbed his assault rifle and gave her ass one last look before going on about his business. The henchmen sat their weapons aside and unzipped their pants, pulling out their throbbing hard dicks. Four of them held down her arms and legs, while the others took turns raping her. She balled her face up, wrinkles forming at the corners of her eyes and around her nose. The queen pin bit down hard on her bottom lip, combating the pain that ripped through her asshole and pussy. Tears formed in her eyes and went running from their corners. Her head jumped up and down, as the lustful grunts and moans of men filled the air. They tried to shove their dicks into her mouths, but she wasn't having that. Hell nah, she whipped her head from left to right, trying her best not to have her mouth violated. Before she knew it she was being punched in the gut and her mouth was involuntarily opening from the pain. Her lips had parted far open enough to have one of their dicks shoved into it. She gagged and her eyelids narrowed into slits. Her pupils rolled up at the man and she scowled, biting down on his hardness. The assault caused the man to scream loud enough to rupture everyone's eardrums. He staggered backwards holding his bleeding semi-limp penis, agony written across his face. Dropping to his ass, he looked to his palms and saw that they were smeared with blood. Hearing her laughing, he got upon his feet and got his M-16. Limping forward and holding his mangled privates with one hand, he made his way over to the victim as his comrades continued to ravage her. Her eyes shot up to their corners observing the man mad dogging her and holding his ruined cock. Gritting, he took his choppa into both hands and slammed the butt of it into her temple, knocking her ass out cold.

Victoria was dead to the world as the henchmen took turns raping every hole of her body. Thank God she was knocked out cold, because there wasn't any way in hell she would want to have been conscious to experience what they were doing to her.

***

Zay looked around nervously as he was driven to the back of a house that was under construction. The Crown Victoria parked underneath the shade of a tree. The only thing that could be heard was the sounds of crickets. Then, there were the doors of the vehicle opening and slamming shut as the D.E.A agents hopped out. The two men made it around to the back of the Crown and popped the trunk, removing extendable batons.

Snap! Snap!

The white men extended the extendable batons and made to bring their suspect harm. Zay's head snapped from left to right trying to see what side the agents were approaching from. His heart pounded inside of his chest and he felt his palms growing sweaty. He didn't know what the fuck these devils had in store for him, but he wasn't about to go out without a fight. That was for damn sure.

"You like to kill agents, huh? Well, we've got something for your…" The tallest agent opened the back door and was rewarded with a hard kick to the face. The impact from the blow sent his baton up into the air and him stumbling backwards fast and hard, crashing to the dirt. Zay hopped right out. As soon as he turned to his left, he was rushed by the shorter of the agents. The chunky man snarled and showcased his coffee stained teeth, swinging his baton from left to right. The cock sucka was trying to bust his mothafucking head wide open. Wrists handcuffed behind his back, Zay moved with the finesse of a ballroom dancer, dodging the threat of the weapon. He avoided the quick swings of the baton, and even managed to leap over his attacker's foot when he tried to sweep kick him. The fight left both combatants sweaty and out of breath.

"Haa! Haa! Haa! Haa!" the chunky agent looked like he was ready to pass out. His eyes looked sleepy and his broad chest rose and fell rapidly.

"Haa! Haa! Haa! Haa!" Zay stared at him, ready for whatever else he may bring, "You 'bout ready to throw in the towel, fat man?"

"Fuck youuuu!" he bellowed, spit flying from off of his thin, chapped lips. He charged at Zay. The muscle headed brute jumped up in the air and did a Round House kick. The impact of his heel slamming into the hefty agent's jaw sent a ripple effect throw the meat of his face. Blood went flying everywhere and his big ass flopping to the ground like a dead fish. Hearing movement at his back, Zay whipped around to see the tallest of the agent getting upon his worn leather shoes. His face was red and the imprint of the bottom of the bandit's boot was on his face. His eyes were glassy and angry, burgundy surrounding his ears. He took the time to wipe the blood that trickled from his nostrils with the back of his hand and looked at the smear that he'd created. When he looked back up, he saw that his suspect was waiting on his next move. The muscle headed brute was waiting on him to swing that god damn baton at him, but, nah, the devil was smarter than that. "Nuh unh, homie," he smiled devilishly and retracted the baton. He stashed it into his belt and pulled his service weapon, a Glock .23 handgun. He gripped it with two hands, and pointed the dangerous end of it at Zay. This caused the bandit to freeze in his tracks, standing up right. There wasn't shit that he could do against a bullet, besides, dying once being struck by it. "Now, you're gone stand right there, while my buddy and I beat shit down your legs."

The tallest agent watched as his moaning comrade scrambled to his feet, picking up his extendable baton. He looked as mad as a bull as he spat blood off to the side. His eyebrows arched and his nose scrunched up.

"Keep your gun on him, LeBlanc, I'm gonna beat this son of a bitch like a runaway slave!" he claimed, stalking forward.

"We both are." He brandished his baton and extended it again, striking Zay upside the head. The muscle headed brute crumbled to the ground and the men pounced on him.

Whack! Crack! Thwack! Wamp!

The D.E.A agents beat the shit out Zay until they were exhausted. They then took a cigarette break and beat his ass some more. The only thing that could be heard that night, besides the crickets, were their suspect's howls of pain and the batons smacking against him.

Chapter Three

As soon as Loon and his young killas crossed the threshold inside of the hospital, they opened up on the security guards. Their AK-47s spat hot fire turning their gray uniform shirts burgundy and splattering the walls with their blood. They spun around and hit the floor wincing and dead. As soon as they met with the linoleum, that crazy mothafuckaz and the youngstas moved to the police. Five-Owe were drawing their weapons, but before they could clear the guns from their holsters they were met with deadly fire. Sharp jacketed bullets went in and out of their forms, causing them to dance on their feet. Their expressions were of unbearable pain as they met with death. The cops fell towards the waxed floor, hitting the surface just as the empty shell casings did. People were running back and forth across their path, screaming and hollering, trying to get the fuck out of the way before they ended up on the wrong side of some bullets.

"Aye, you, come here!" Loon called out, pointing his assault rifle at the fleeing desk clerk. She'd just came from behind her desk and was running. "Bitch, you keep running and I'll spray yo' ass down." He swore. The threat made her freeze in her tracks. Trembling, she lifted her hands in the air and slowly turned around to him, looking like she was on the verge of tears. Curling and uncurling his finger, he called her over to him. She hesitantly approached, people running across her front and back. "I needa know what room Clarence Spivey is in."

The clerk nodded and looked up the name that she was given, "Room 321, on the 5th floor." She reported her findings.

"Thank you."

Blaaat!

Loon smiled wickedly after shooting her in the chest. She collapsed to the floor and he went on about his business. He and his cleanup crew whacked out the remaining security guards and sheriffs on their way to the elevator lobby, reloading their AK-47s. They boarded the elevator as soon as the double doors opened. The doors closed and Loon pressed the number of the floor that he was looking for.

Hearing screams and rapid gunfire, a wincing Gar peeled himself from off of the bed. With narrowed eyelids, he gave his surroundings a quick scan and realized that he was inside of a hospital. Taking in his appearance, he saw the gown, the medical machinery that he was hooked up to, and the band around his wrist. He went to get out of bed and pain shot throughout his entire body. His face balled up in agony. That's when the imagery of him being blasted on flew back and forth across his mental. He was in the beginning stages of feeling his wounds with the morphine having started to wear off. Taking a deep breath, he pulled off all of the patches that were attached to him and removed his I.V. Next, he took off the breathing tube and slung it aside. Throwing his legs over the side of the bed, he hopped down and he fell awkwardly. His legs felt like cooked noodles underneath him. He landed hard on his face, busting his mouth and chipping his front tooth. He lay there for a time, but once he heard more gunfire, he pushed up from off of the shiny floor. Looking down and seeing his reflection, he spat out slimy blood. Afterwards, he tried to pull himself up by grabbing the side of his bed, but his legs weren't having it. Having grown angry and frustrated, he looked back at his uncooperative limbs.

"Work goddamn you, you mothafuckaz, goddamn you!" he cursed them, red spittle flying from off of his lips. Calming down, he shut his eyes and took a deep breath to prepare himself for the battle he knew he was going to face. Once he got a grip on things, he crawled out into the hallway. He'd just crossed the threshold, when he heard more rapidly gunfire and screams. Looking down the hallway, he saw some of the hospital staff, patients and visitors running his way. He stuck his hand out and pleaded with them to help him, but they didn't say shit. Nah, they just kept on running for their lives. Seeing a lone man in a wheelchair rolling his way and frequently glancing over his shoulder, Gar realized that this was his chance at salvation and he'd be damned if he missed it. Turning to his left he saw a mop leaning against the wall out of a yellow bucket. Quickly grabbing it, he looked to the man in the wheelchair and saw that he was none the wiser to his presence, which was perfect for him. Gar focused his attention on the spinning wheels of the wheelchair. He took the mop by its handle and licked his lips, timing the spinning wheels of the chair. They looked like blurs rolling past him, but he had a watchful eye. Quietly, he waited for his chance and then reacted, shoving the handle into one of the spinning blades. This action stopped the wheelchair in its tracks and caused its passenger to go flying from where he was perched.

"Got 'em," Gar announced, seeing the damage that his actions had caused. He tossed the mop handle aside and crawled over to the nigga that had been propelled from out of the chair. The wheelchair bound man move to get upon his feet and Gar saw an opportunity to make advantage of. He jabbed him in the throat with his extended fingers and he grabbed his neck. Next, he was poked in his eyes, punched in the nuts and then cracked across the jaw fast. He fell out, lying on his back snoring unconscious. Seeing this, Gar pulled himself upon the wheelchair and sat down, people running past him on either side of him. They were all sweating and wearing scared expressions on their faces. Some of the people bumped into the wheelchair. This caused some of them to fall and others to stumble. Either way, they kept on going because they didn't want to be laid down by gunfire.

Blatatatatatatatatatatatatatatat!

Blatatatatatatatatatatatatatatat!

Gar rolled off as fast as he could, hearing the gunfire growing closer and closer. Rolling away, he glanced over his shoulder and saw sheriffs backup down the hallway, hands extending their guns. They squeezed off shot after shot, taking some of their own in the process. They began falling in a domino effect, howling in pain as they caught bullets in the parts of them that weren't protected by bulletproof vests. Once law enforcement crumbled to the linoleum, Loon and his young killas moved in and finished them off.

Blatatatatatatatatatatatatatatat!

Blatatatatatatatatatatatatatatat!

Blood and brain fragments went flying everywhere, smacking against the wall and sliding down it. Having made short work of the badges, the AK-47 toting trio made their way down the hallway in Gar's direction. When he saw their asses, his eyelids snapped wide open and his hearted pounded like an African drum. Seeing that his life was hanging in the balance, he rolled as fast as he could in the wheelchair, panting out of breath. Loon and the young killas stopped to take a shot at Gar, but the people surrounding him made it extremely difficult.

"Fuck it! Spray 'em all." Loon ordered his hittas.

"All of 'em?" Cuba asked to be sure.

"All 'em!" he projected louder and they opened up on everyone in the stampede. Screams and hollers bounced off of the walls inside of the hallway. Bodies and smoking shell casing hit the floor, some of them deflecting off of the tip of the shooters sneakers. Gar ducked down as low as he could, rolling down the hallway. The nigga looked like a blur as fast as his ass was flying down the corridor. The doors of nearby rooms slammed shut as people ducked off into them, leaving some of the people on the outside pounding on them trying to get in.

Bang! Bang! Bang! Bang!

The fists of scared patients and visitors pummeled the doors, causing them to rattle.

"Open up!" One man hollered out.

"Oh, my God, please, let us in!" another man hollered out.

"Pleeease!" a woman hollered.

Bang! Bang! Bang! Bang!

The fists continued to pummel the doors. Seeing the trio of shooters still coming, the scared people took off running, some of them being cut down by rapid gunfire. They hollered in agony as hot metal ripped through their backs and limbs, spotting up the walls and floor with blood.

"Haa! Haa! Haa! Haa!" Gar took the time to wipe his sweaty brows with the back of his hand as he continued to roll down the corridor. He repeatedly glanced over his shoulder, seeing innocent people being cut down by rapid fire. They appeared to be falling over dead right behind him. He felt sorry for them, but he was grateful to still have his life. Having turned back around from glancing over his shoulder, Gar found two sheriffs that had run from out of the staircase door. The two law enforcers pointed their weapons at Loon and his killas, popping off. The sound of gunfire filled the air and empty shell casing went flying everywhere. One of the sheriffs is taken down by a wave of quick fire, while one danced on feet, taking heated bullets. Gar rolled towards the dancing sheriff full speed ahead. He brought all of his weight down on the front of his wheelchair, and propelled himself from it, tackling the dancing law enforcer to the floor. He flipped over the dead body and snatched up his gun. He then rolled forward and kicked the staircase door open with all of his might. He shot up ducking and running. Throwing himself through the doorway, he landed on his back just as the young killas ran into the doorway, pointing their choppas at his ass. Gar slid down the steps of the staircase on his back aiming his banger at the hittas, blazing at them.

Pop! Pop! Pop! Pop!

Cuba and Biggie ducked down out of the way, narrowly missing the bullets. When they came back up to return fire, Gar was flipping over onto the landing and running to the staircase of the next floor. Loon had just come through the door when he disappeared. He switched hands with the choppa and motioned for his young killas to follow him. Together they went after Gar.

Gar ran down the corridor going from door to door, twisting their knobs. Realizing that they were all locked and hearing hurried footsteps coming down the hallway, he looked to his left and found a place for him to escape. Although he didn't want to do what he had in mind, he really didn't have a choice. He was trapped, and the idea he had in mind was his only salvation. Loon and his young killas had just made it to the hallway that he was inside of, when he'd taken off running. His heart beat wildly, flooding his ears. He huffed and puffed, chest rising and falling fast. He'd made it to the balcony; he did a cartwheel over it and turned his gun on them. He narrowed his eyelids and opened fire on them, trigger finger squeezing rapidly.

Pop! Pop! Pop!

Loon and his killas ducked and scrambled to avoid the dangerous bullets hurling towards them, missing them by mere inches. Debris and particles flew every which way. Loon and his killas assembled at the corridor and pointed their assault rifles, spitting flames. Their projectiles missed their intended target as he fell out of sight. They exchanged glances at one another, looking shocked, mouths wide open. They knew in their hearts that homeboy was dead, but they had to see for themselves. Loon lowered his choppa and motioned for his killas to follow him as he crept towards the balcony. Lowering their weapons, they cautiously moved in on the balcony, wind blowing against them and ruffling their clothing. Loon tapped Biggie and pointed to the balcony, signaling for him to see what had become of their enemy. Having given his big homie a nod, Biggie eased towards the balcony and looked over its edge. When he looked downward, he found Gar hanging from the edge of the balcony below. His face was balled up and he was pointing his banger up at him, pulling back on the trigger.

Pop!

Splat!

A single bullet blew through Biggie's forehead and exploded out the back of his skull. Brain fragments, pieces of skull, and chunks of his scalp still attached to his nappy hair went flying everywhere. Biggie's dead weight fell onto the edge of the balcony. His eyes stared out into space and his arms dangled about, blood dripping from the gaping hole inside of his forehead. Once he killed over, Loon and that nigga Cuba ran over to the edge and looked down. Cuba's eyes were glassy and hurt having lost his best friend and crime partner. He shrilled in emotional pain and pointed his assault rifle down at Gar, him and Loon's crazy ass. They opened fire on Gar, just as his hand released the edge. He fell backwards. Freefalling, he gripped his steel with both hands and pointed at the fools that were blazing at him. Bullets whizzed past him as he let off, round after round.

Pop! Pop! Pop!

Loon and Cuba ducked and scrambled from out of Gar's line of fire. Hunched down behind the balcony, Loon and his lone killa exchanged knowing glances. Giving one another a head nod, they jumped up and looked over the balcony. Scowling, they swayed their assault rifles back and forth firing them. Their eyes snapped open with shock when they saw that their enemy had vanished. They were expecting him to have fallen to his death.

"Where the fuck this nigga go?" Loon's head swept back and forth across his surroundings. He didn't see Gar anywhere in sight.

"I…I don't know, it's like the mothafucka just vanished." A confused expression was on Cuba's face.

Hearing police car sirens and seeing a stampede of people hopping into their respective vehicles, Loon tapped his little homie and they took off, not wanting to get caught.

***

A terrified white lady sat stiff behind the wheel of her white on white Audi, she occasionally sniffled and wiped her eyes with the back of her hand. The entire time she was driving she was glancing into the rearview mirror at the person that had abducted her. She couldn't see him, but she could feel him. Well, not him, but his gun, which was pressed to the side of her skull.

"All right, Martha, you're doing beautifully." Gar commented on her driving. He was slumped low in the backseat on the Dodge Neon, his banger ready to blow her head off if she didn't mind him. As soon as she paid the parking fee and the barrier lifted for her to leave, he took his tool from her head. She sighed with relief but she knew that her ass wasn't out of the fire yet. Nah, she had a scary looking black man riding in the backseat of her car with the gun, and she didn't know what the fuck his plan for her was.

A wincing Gar looked at his left leg. It was broken, its red bone poking out of the side of it. It was bruised black and bluish purple and oozing blood. Looking at his nasty wound, he couldn't help remembering how he'd gotten it not long ago.

Flashback

Gar flipped over as he hurled towards the ground, eyelids stretched wide open and limbs swinging wildly. His hospital gown ruffled from the air blowing up against it. He out-stretched his foot as he reached the surface, snap.

"Ahhhhhhhhh!" he wailed like a wounded animal, break-ing his leg and falling to the ground. The side of his face smacked up against the ground and his gun skidded across the surface. He whimpered in agony, peeling his eyelids open and seeing what looked like one thousand pairs of sneakers and shoes running across his line of vision. The panicked cries and screams of the people of the hospital filled the air, they were tripping and falling over each other, trying to get the fuck from up out of there. Having forced the pain into the back of his mind, Gar snatched up his weapon and hopped upon his good leg. He looked from left to right, seeing vehicles flee the parking lot and people running for their lives. Hearing a speeding car heading into his direction, he hobbled around on

one foot and pointed his blazer at the driver behind the windshield. The Caucasian lady sitting behind the wheel looked surprised. She slammed on the brakes and brought her car to a squealing halt. Keeping his strap on her, Gar hobbled around to the driver side window. He ordered her to pop the locks and then he hopped into the backseat, slamming the door shut behind him.

"What's your name?" he asked, pressed that plastic/steel against the back of her melon.

"Mar…Martha." She stammered terrified. The tears couldn't stop falling from her eyes; she was visibly shaken up by the entire ordeal.

"You got lil'ones, Martha?"

"Y…Yes." She nodded, then wiped her eyes with the back of her hand which wore her wedding band.

"You wanna live to see 'em again?"

"Yes…Yes, I do."

"Good. You get me outta here, and I'll make sure this all seems like one big nightmare, okay?"

"Okay." She nodded and wiped her eyes again, mashing on the gas pedal and taking off at a moderate speed. While she drove off, Gar's head was on a swivel making sure that no one was witnessing what was going on. There wasn't a pair of eyes focused on them. Everyone was occupied with trying to

get the fuck out of dodge before they ended up catching a couple of hot ones.

Present

"Jesus," Gar made the ugliest face a man could make in a lot of pain. He then sat up with his back against the back door, gripping his handgun. He had tears in his eyes and his leg looked like it was throbbing. "Pull over some place dark, okay?"

"Wait, I thought you said I was going to live through this?" she panicked and whined, shedding more tears.

"Relax, fucking relax, goddamn it. I'm not gonna pop you." He assured her. "I just want to go some place where no one can see us exchanging positions. You got that?"

"You promise?"

"My right hand before God." He held up his hand palm showing.

"All right."

Gar took a deep breath and laid his head back against the back door. He shut his eyelids briefly and took a deep breath. His face wrinkled feeling the excruciation shoot up and down his damaged leg. The street lights illuminated the inside of the vehicle, but it slowly darkened the further they drove. The next thing he knew they were pulling over and Martha was turning off the engine. "Gemme your driver's license and social security card." She obliged him. "Now, I want chu to climb over into the front passenger seat. And please, don't try to run 'cause I'll shoot chu dead in yo' fucking back." He held up his gun for her to see it.

"Don't worry, I'm not gonna try anything." She said, climbing over into the front passenger seat. Hearing him grunting and hollering trying to climb out of the backseat and into the driver's seat, she looked over her shoulder and saw that beads of sweat had accumulated over his face. She also noticed the shininess on his forearms and the how badly hurt his leg was. This caused her face to ball up; she cringed and turned her face.

"You…You need some…some help?" she asked timidly.

"Yeah, take this." He passed her the gun; she took it and watched him climb over into the driver seat. When he finally settled down sweat was dripping from his brows so he wiped it away with the back of his fist. Once he turned around he saw Martha holding the handgun on him, he looked from the gun up to her. His eyes said to go ahead and pull the trigger, but surprisingly, she handed back to her. He then pressed it to her forehead and pulled the trigger, it clicked. Her eyes widen and her heart got caught in her throat. She shuddered, thinking that she almost died.

"Get outta here, Martha." Gar ordered her. She hopped out of the car and ran in the opposite direction. Once he saw that she was gone, he sat his gun in his lap and drove off.

***

"Fuck!" Loon slammed his fist into the ceiling of his car. "Fuck! Fuck! Fuck!" his fist came back to back angrily. Holding his ski-mask in his hand, which he'd just pulled off, he repeatedly glanced over his shoulder until he was several blocks away from the hospital. "We had 'em, we fucking had 'em. We were this close, this close," he held his index and thumb a half an inch apart.

"Yeah, but now we hot. I mean, real hot." Cuba said from behind the wheel, glancing back and forth between the rear-view mirror and the windshield.

"Ain't no need to wet it 'cause we were masked up." He took the time to light up his half smoked blunt.

"True dat, big homie, but we left Biggie back there. He's the only one left that's linking us…well, me, to the massacre back there."

"Fuck you mean?" he asked, having threw his head back and blown out smoke.

"What I'm sayin' is the opps know Biggie is a well known associate of mine. They could come lookin' for me to ask questions."

He shrugged and said, "Big fucking deal. If them crackas come knocking you tell 'em you don't know jack shit. It's as simple as that."

"I'ma needa alibi."

"No shit. Get ta thinking of one." He focused his attention out of the window.

There was silence and then Cuba spoke again, "Where are we going now?"

"We needa get rid of this fucking car and these burners." He blew smoke from out of his nostrils and mouth.

"All right then, that's where it's at."

Loon and Cuba threw their AK-47s into the gutter. They then had Loon's bitch meet them on Eleventh Avenue where there was several warehouses that had been closed for quite some time. Once the homie's girl pulled up, they set the getaway car ablaze and jumped into her whip. They drove away from the catastrophe just as the getaway car exploded, sending burning wreckage everywhere.

Chapter Four

Zay lay on the cold floor of the holding cell, wincing as he touched his battered and swollen face. The two agents had done a real number on him, he was aching all over. Not to mention, his eye was swollen shut, his nose was bruised and his lips were busted. That was the least of his problems though, considering the fact that he'd bodied a D.E.A agent.

When Zay brought his hand down from his face, he remembered the day that both of his hands were hideously burned. Back then he was a young nigga, about eighteen years old. He was strung out on heroine and pulling licks with his sister's crew. They were a ragtag bunch that would do just about anything for a dollar. Anyway, one particular night they'd just made off with a pretty decent score. After they'd done their thang they headed back to their rally point to divide the spoils.

Flashback

The basement was dark, save for the lone light bulb dangling from the string above the table. It illuminated everyone gathered at the table. KeKe, Angelique, and Zay watched Maine run the racks through a money-counter. Maine dipped his hand in and out of a pillowcase. He'd pop the rubber-band on the racks and drop them into the machine. He'd then sit back and watch the money-counter do its job. Once it was done he'd repeat this procedure.

"That's 160 bands, so that's 40K apiece." Maine announced once the machine finished counting the racks. Afterwards, he separated the money for each individual in his crew. He stacked the racks neatly on top of each other and pushed them in front of the man and women that made up his crew.

KeKe, Angelique and Zay broke out with sacks of their very own and pulled their earnings into them, dropping it off into their sacks. They then pulled the drawstrings on them and set them aside.

"So, oh fearless leader," Angelique lit up a cigarette and propped her boots upon the table. "When is our next gig?"

"I've gotta few things lined up but they aren't about shit." Maine admitted. "They'd pay even less than this caper we pulled off tonight."

"I ain't stunting it," Angelique shrugged like it wasn't a big deal. As long as it was a dollar to be made she was going to make her business to get it. "When you talking about paper you hitting my G-spot, cash keep the coochie wet."

"You ain't never lied." KeKe added.

Angelique glanced at KeKe and rolled her eyes. She didn't like her. This was because she'd stolen Maine right from under her nose. It didn't even matter to her that she and Maine weren't exclusive. As far as she was concerned, they were fucking so that made him hers.

"I hear you. I'ma 'bout mine, too," Maine told her. "But I don't wanna keep putting our asses out there for this short paper. I want that big score that'll have us sitting pretty for a while, ya feel me? If we're gonna risk our lives then let it be for the high stakes."

KeKe and Zay nodded their heads understanding where Maine was coming from. Angelique on the other hand wasn't trying to hear that.

"Fuck all of that, I got bills to pay." Angelique waved him off.

"We all do." Maine reminded her with an attitude. "We do these hits as a squad, so we can watch one another's backs, but anytime you feel like you don't wanna be a part of this ensemble...you can walk."

"I hear that hot shit." Angelique smirked and licked her lips. She took her boots from off of the table top and sat up. "With that said, I'll be taking my leave." She put the cigarette between her lips and snatched up her sack. On her way to the staircase she stopped and looked at Zay. "Some trap boy is

going to cake off something real nice these next couple of days, ain't that right, Zay?"

"Stay the fuck outta my business, Angelique." Zay said, not bothering to turn around. By the look on his face you could tell that his habit was wreaking havoc on him. "What I do with my take doesn't concern you."

"You know the rest of us actually put in work for our share, right?" Angelique asked him.

Zay turned around in his chair and said, "And I don't?"

Angelique twisted her lips and tilted her head to the side, "Nigga, you ain't nothing but a glorified chauffeur. If you can't see that, you need to shoot your ass down to Lens Crafters."

Zay shot to his feet heatedly. The anger etched upon his face made it clear that he wasn't feeling what Angelique was saying.

KeKe stood to her feet ready to defend her baby brother but a wave of his hand made her fallback. He was a grown ass man and didn't want his big sister fighting his battles like she'd done when he was a kid.

"I'ma getaway driver," Zay told Angelique, "My job is just as important as everyone else's."

"Angelique, I think you'd better be taking your leave now." Maine spoke up.

Angelique lifted her hand. "Nah, my nigga, junior here needs to hear this." She kept her eyes casted in Zay's direction. "The only reason why Maine's been keeping you on is 'cause he's laying the pipe to your sister. If it wasn't for that your burnt-out ass would be out here looking to turn in shopping carts of scrap metal for your next fix, like the rest of the dope fiends."

"Angelique," Maine barked, shooting to his feet; she ignored that nigga though.

"Maine won't tell you that he doesn't want chu in the thick of things with the rest of us holding them bangers 'cause he's scared you'll be too geeked up to watch his back and is afraid that one of us will end up getting peeled as a result."

While Angelique was shooting off at the mouth, Zay looked over his shoulder at Maine who just shook his head, denying her claims. Zay then focused his attention back on Angelique.

"The truth is my nigga feels sorry for you." Angelique divulged. "He knows that there isn't a jack boy in The Bottoms that's dumb enough to pull a job with chu. So he throws you a bone and gives you some story about how badly he needs you on his team with your superior driving skills. Sheeiiit, you good but mothafucka you aren't that good. I could handle a strap and the driving if it's gone save us a couple of grand."

"That's how y'all feel?" Zay looked from Angelique to Maine with hurt in his eyes. She'd cut him deeper than any straight razor could.

"Zay, it ain't even like that, homie. We're all family here." Maine tried to convince him but the truth of the matter was everything Angelique had revealed was true. But there wasn't any way that he was going to tell that to Zay because he had love for the little nigga. He looked at him as if he was his little brother.

Zay waved him off and casted his eyes on KeKe.

"What about you, sis? You feel the same?"

KeKe just hung her head; she was just as guilty as the rest of them when it came about Zay's dealing in the crew. But saying so would destroy him, so she'd much rather remain tight lipped on the subject.

"Your silence is enough." Zay blinked and hot tears shot down his face. He quickly wiped his face with the back of his fist. He threw on his hood and snatched up his sack. "Y'all don't gotta worry about Zay no more, 'cause from now on a nigga getting it how he lives on his own. Duces," He chucked up two fingers and moved for the steps, making sure to bump Angelique's shoulder on his way up the staircase. She gave him a look that could kill as he headed up the staircase.

"Zay, come back," KeKe called after him. "Angelique doesn't speak for the rest of us!"

"The fuck I don't, you got it on your mind just like me and Maine do." Angelique told her. "Difference is, I got the balls to say what y'all don't," her eyes shifted from Maine to KeKe. "Face it KeKe, your baby brotha is dead weight. I just did us a favor. I just freed up a few more bands for us to split. But, aye, if you're in your feelings about it we can settle it right now."

"Don't talk about it, be about it." KeKe pulled off her sweatshirt, revealing the wife beater she wore underneath it. She tossed the sweatshirt aside and mad dogged Angelique as she cracked the knuckles on both of her hands.

"That's what I'm talking about, baby girl. Fuck all of this lip boxing."

Angelique dropped her sack and spat into her palm. She then snuffed the ember of her cigarette out in her spit. She tucked the square behind her ear and pulled off her hoodie.

KeKe started for Angelique but a slab of dark flesh moved into her path, blocking her line of vision. She looked up and saw that she was at Maine's back.

"Keep that shit moving, Angelique; I'm not having no bullshit at the spot," Maine told her, clutching his Desert Eagle. Angelique started to defy him but the glint in his eyes

made her fallback. She knew that look all too well. It wasn't seen until he was ready to take an altercation to a level where either he or someone else would end up dead.

"You got this one." Angelique told KeKe as she slipped her hoodie back on, "But one day Daddy won't be there to save you."

"Save me. Bitch he just rescued you from a thorough ass beating." KeKe moved to harm Angelique, but Maine throwing his arm across her chest held her fast. "I swear 'fore God, Angelique, you got one more time to buck on me and I'ma whip you 'til you catch on fire, ya hear me, hoe?"

"Oh, I'ma do more than buck, please believe me. And when I do you gone have to show and prove." Angelique said.

"Toodles," She kissed her palm and blew KeKe a kiss, taunting her. KeKe tried to break free so she could put her foot in her ass, but Maine had a Death Lock around her she couldn't break.

"Oooooooh, I fucking hate that bitch," KeKe roared.

"The feeling is mutual, honey." Angelique said over her shoulder, heading towards the staircase. She had just planted her boot on the first step when she got a surprise.

Whoomp!

Zay came tumbling down the staircase fast, landing on the floor. He lay there wincing and rolling from side to side. When

Maine, KeKe and Angelique saw Zay tumbling down the staircase like that they went to pull their weapons, but Mabel came running down the staircase with a chrome shotgun. He pointed the powerful weapon at Angelique and then Maine and KeKe, ordering them to toss their weapons to the ground, which they did.

"Any one of y'all niggaz move and that's ya ass!" Mabel warned, pointing the shotgun around at all of them. There was silence as he eye fucked each and every one of them. "Flip the table over!"

Maine, KeKe and Angelique didn't move a muscle. They just stood there mad dogging homeboy. It wasn't until he racked his shotgun that Maine took it upon himself to flip the table over. The action sent the sacks of money falling to the floor. Once this was done, Mabel whistled and someone slowly descended the staircase, causing the steps to squeak one by one. The gang saw the lower half of him, which were in black jeans and boots. When he finally made it down to the landing, they got a full scope of him. It was Derek. He was a lanky nigga that kept his hair in cornrows that reached just past his ear. He had a thin goatee and wide nostrils. In his earlobes he sported small diamond earrings. He wore a see-through oxygen mask over his nose and mouth, which was attached to the oxygen tanks that were laying snuggly inside of a black bag that hung off of his shoulder. He stood before the quartet patting an aluminum baseball bat into his palm.

"Well, well, well, long time no…" Derek looked down and saw a wincing Zay at his feet. "I remember this lil' nigga, hold this," he kicked him in the side. "And this," he kicked him in the side again and then stomped his head. Afterwards, he spit on his face and looked to Mabel. "Tie these mothafuckaz up, man. I'll keep 'em under the gun," he snatched his chrome shotgun and pointed at Maine. The gang stayed where they were with their hands up in the air, allowing Mabel to gag and bound their wrists. He then watched him plant them in their chairs. Having finished the task at hand, Mabel walked off lighting up a blunt and blowing out smoke.

Maine, KeKe, Angelique and Zay sat in a circle in a way that they could see one another. They squirmed around and tried to talk, but the gags in their mouths prohibited it. Their eyelids were also stretched wide open, held in place by duct-tape. Their backs were left in the dark but their faces were in the center of light that the dangling bulb above provided. Derek slowly walked around the circle with his baseball bat lying on his shoulder. He smiled wickedly as he circled the quartet, making a three hundred and sixty degree turn around them. Off in the shadows of the basement was Mabel, shotgun hanging at his side as he took pulls from his bleezy. Its ember glowing in the dark with each drag he took from the end of it.

"Well, I guess I betta get started."

With a grunt, Derek brought the baseball bat down with all of his might. Upon impact of Angelique's skull, it made a noise that sounded like a giant egg cracking open. Instantly, blood came running down her face and her eyes rolled up to the ceiling. Maine, KeKe and Zay cringed, but kept watching in horror. Angelique's aggressor didn't show any remorse. He didn't give a fuck about her being a woman. The second time the bat came down, more blood ran and her eyeball nearly popped out of its socket. The third time sent blood splattering on Maine, KeKe and Zay's faces. They squeezed their eyelids shut, listening to their crime partner being brutally beaten. Derek swung his bat down over and over again, sending more blood flying and running down Angelique's face. She was still now, taking the merciless pounding from the aluminum bat. Exhausted, Derek swung his baseball bat down at his side and looked over his handiwork. His chest jumped up and down fast, observing the mess he'd created.

"You've got blood on your face." Mabel told him.

"What did you say?" Derek looked over his shoulder at his man.

his man.

Mabel snatched the blunt out of his mouth so what he was saying would be clear. "I said, 'you've got blood on your face, nigga."

"Oh...thanks." He turned back around and wiped the blood from off of his face. "Now, where was I? Oh, now I remember." He walked around the chairs, taking in all of their occupants faces. Maine, KeKe and Zay mad dogged his ass, hating him for what he'd done to their comrade. Tears built up in KeKe's eyes and came sliding down her cheeks. She didn't fuck with Angelique like that, but she didn't want to see the bitch get done dirty either. She just wanted to give her those hands, not kill her crazy ass. As Derek circled his potential victims, their hearts thudded inside of their chests. Although they knew the game they played came with consequences, they never thought in a million years they'd go out like this. Derek stopped at the backs of KeKe and Maine. Their eyes stared out of their corners and their hearts continuously thudded. They tried yelling something at their attacker, but the gags in their mouths wouldn't allow it. Zay's eyes darted back and forth between his sister and her man wondering who would be next to die.

"My man, you're the leader of this outfit, right?" Derek patted Maine's shoulder.

"Fuck you, fuck you, fuck you!" Maine tried to shout through the gag in his mouth, rocking back and forth in his chair, nearly tipping it over.

"That's what I thought." Derek raised the baseball bat above his head and swung it downward, cracking Maine in the skull. When he drew the baseball bat back and his victim's head bobbled, blood flooded his face. He tried to say something, but nobody inside of the basement could understand him.

Crack! Crackk! Crackkk!

KeKe and Zay tried to squeeze their eyes shut but the duct-tape wouldn't allow that shit. Nah, they had to watch.

Derek swung his bat down repeatedly, sending blood flying everywhere. Specks clung to his face, clothes, sneakers and everyone else. Madness danced in his eyes as he continued to strike down upon his victim with vengeance and furious anger. His shadow was casted on the wall as he handled his business, his brother watching from the shadows and smoking his blunt. Once he was done with the blunt, he dropped what was left of it on the floor and mashed it out under his sneaker. He kept his eyes on Derek as he blew smoke out into the air, watching him bring the bat down to his side.

"That shit looks nasty than a mothafucka." A disgusted expression came across Derek's face, seeing blood and brain

fragments ooze out the top of that nigga, Maine's skull. He then looked to his brother, pointing to the mess he'd created. "Say, bruh, you ever seen some shit like this before?"

"Plenty of times, man. Now, finish these fools off so we can get in the wind." Mabel responded annoyed.

"Keep your panties on, nigga, you see me working. I'll be done in a minute shit." Derek stepped behind KeKe, tears ran down her face. She was crying for herself, Maine, and her brother, Zay. She knew she couldn't stop death from coming so she egged it on, screaming at the top of her lungs and rocking her seat. "Bye, bye, lil' birdie."

Crack! Crackk! Crackkk! Crackkkk!

Blow after blow rained down on KeKe's head, blood and pieces of her brain smacked up against her killa's face. This didn't stop him though; he kept right ahead with his order of business. Zay tried to shout at him, but the gag stopped any words from escaping his lips. He struggled to get out of his chair, tilting it from left to right until it eventually fell. Lying where he was, he cried, watching his older sister getting pummeled to hamburger meat. Once her killa was done, he tossed the baseball bat aside and walked over to him. As his brother began splashing the basement with gasoline, Derek went on to talk to Zay.

"You, you're gonna get it worse than them all, it's 'cause of you that I'm hooked up to this fuckin' tank," he shook the bag at him that held his oxygen tank. His eyes were glassy and menacing. He adjusted the strap of the bag on his shoulder as he glared down at Zay, who was making an ugly ass face and crying his eyes out. The dead faces of his sister and comrades hurt his heart. Derek didn't give a fuck though. Them niggaz had harmed him and he had to get at them for what they had done.

Mabel emptied out the gas can and threw it aside. He pulled out a book of matches and tore out a match stick. Once he swept the head of the match across the black strip, a flame hissed to life, licking the air.

"It's time for us to go." Mabel announced to his bald head crime partner.

Derek and Zay were now locked into an intense stare mad dogging one another. Derek's eyes danced with madness, while Zay's were red webbed and running with tears. The youth slightly shook as he clenched his fists, dying to get out of his restraints and put hands on that mothafucka for killing his loved ones.

"Derek!"

"Hold your fuckin' horses, Mabel!" Derek called out over his shoulder and then looked back to the youth. "Here's one to

grow on, sport!" he kicked Zay in his stomach hard as shit and knocked the wind out of him. He eyes bulged and he coughed harder and harder, wincing. Derek then went about his business, walking back towards his brother and heading back up the staircase. He was halfway up the steps once Mabel tossed the match and came up after him. As soon as the flaming match mingled with the gasoline, fire swept throughout the basement. Before Zay knew it he found the basement hot and himself growing sweaty by the second. He tried his damndest to get free of his restraints and up from off of the floor but his efforts weren't of any use. Looking down at his sneakers, Zay saw a line of fire heading his way. His eyes stretched wide open and he gasped. He kicked and squirmed, but it wasn't enough to get free.

"Raaaaah!" he threw his head back hollering loud enough to bust someone's eardrums. Tears accumulated in his eyes and ran down his cheeks. He struggled harder and faster, dancing where he was lying on the floor. The fire had engulfed his sneakers and was eating up his back. Zay continued to holler and cry out, struggling to get away from the fire that was sizzling his flesh. Before he knew it he felt the tape growing weaker and weaker, until, finally, he tore loose from the tape. Hurriedly, he jumped to his feet and ran over to an old dirty blanket in the corner of the basement that had

cobwebs on it. He draped the blanket over himself and snuffed out the flames, including the ones that had engulfed his foot wear. Having thrown the blanket aside, he looked at his hands and arms. They were hideously burned and aching like hell. Dropping his arms to his sides, he looked up and saw his comrades laid out. Running over to his sister, he kneeled down and swept her eyes shut with his hand. Next, he kissed her on the side of her head. Scooping her up into his arms, he carried her up the stairs and kicked the door open. The door swung open and banked off of the wall, giving view to a living room that looked like a raging inferno. Sitting his sister on an area of the floor that wasn't burning, Zay grabbed a ruined iron chair and hurled it through the large window of the living room. The chair imploded out of the opposite side sending shards raining down on the dirt patched lawn. Picking his sister back up, the youth ran towards the broken out window and leaped through it. He hit the ground, dropping his sister, and rolling out. He found himself lying flat on his back and staring up at the stars, breathing hard. His chest jumped up and down with each breath that he took. Sitting up, he was just in time to see a long, black on black Cadillac Deville with limo tinted windows. Although he couldn't see through the windows something in his gut told him that it was Derek and Mabel.

Once Zay had buried his loved ones and his wounds hand healed, he jumped back out in the streets looking for the cock suckas involved in his street family's murder. In his search he discovered that Derek had ended up dying in a car accident, while Mabel got knocked for a couple of bodies. Back then, word on the streets was the nigga was looking at the death penalty.

This didn't go over well with Zay because he'd never get his revenge. He knew that it was something that he would have to grow to accept and eventually he did.

With his loved ones gone, Zay picked right back up where they'd left off, but he chose not to take on a crime partner. Nah, he got out there in the streets by himself robbing and stealing like it was going out of style. Over time he built quite the reputation in the streets. Niggaz feared and respected the jack boy known as Zay. They gave him a wide berth and didn't fuck with him. Mothafuckaz knew better.

Present

Zay seemed to be staring at his burned hands for what seemed like an eternity. He balled his fingers and made fists, turning them over on the opposite side. Dropping his arms at his sides, he stared up at the ceiling. He couldn't help wondering what La'Chat was doing at the moment.

Chapter Five

La'Chat stood beside her bed looking down at her stomach and rubbing it, thinking about the life growing inside of her. A smile was stretched across her lips. She was visibly happy despite her harsh reality. La'Chat had been nauseated and throwing up like a sick god damn dog. At first she thought she had food poisoning, but something at the back of her mind told her that she might be pregnant. So she took a pregnancy test right before her and Zay had met up with that nigga Easy to make the drop. She was going to tell him on their way over but she thought it could wait until they collected the money for the kilos. Unfortunately, she never got the chance to break the good news to him because of the sting.

La'Chat had to pinch herself because she couldn't believe that she was pregnant. She had never thought about being a parent because she was so caught up in the street life. The life she lived was fast and dangerous; definitely not something you'd want to raise a kid in. But now the idea of being a mother didn't seem so bad to her.

Anyway, La' Chat started hoping for a baby boy. She wanted him to be the spitting image of his father. She wanted him to have walk, talk and act like Zay. She wanted him to have the same personality traits and mannerisms as him too. There wasn't any doubt in her mind that if she did give birth to a boy that he would be a junior. The only thing she didn't want was for him to be involved in the streets. Under no circumstances did she want him getting his the ski-mask way like her and his father. Sure she chose the life she led, but she really didn't have any other choice.

Flashback

When La'Chat was twelve years old she was abducted from the L.A County Zoo while on a class field trip. She was taken to the basement of a big house by a meth dealer named Chet. It was there she was chained up to the wall by a metal neck bracelet like some fucking dog. Two bowls were set out for her. One was water and the other was bread and corn beef hash. She was made to shave her head bald and wear a lime green bikini. She was given a bath every two days and hygiene products. A bucket for her to piss and shit in was placed in the far corner of the room. A plastic box of dolls and other toys were also placed down inside of the basement with her. The box was sat beside a mat, a pillow and a small box television set.

Chet didn't seem so bad to La'Chat then. For the past week she ate, played and got to stay up late watching anything she wanted. That was until Sunday night came around and he came down the staircase while she was watching Honey, I shrunk the kids. The sick bastard stood in the shadows, with only the lens of his glasses being seen. This was from the street light post shining in through the small basement window, reflecting on them. La'Chat sat up where she lay and strained her eyes trying to see who it was, calling out to him. He didn't answer though. Nah, the disgusting mothafucka stepped forth dressed in a stringy blonde wig and a black leather bondage suit and pattern leather hooker boots. His gloved hands held tight to a black leather whip that appeared to be ten feet long. Abruptly, he lashed La'Chat and she screamed to the high heavens, voice deflecting off of the walls in the confine space. When he drew back, she had a bloody diagonal line going across her chest and her under developed breasts were left exposed.

Chet grunted with each and every lashing he gave his prisoner, leaving bleeding cuts all over her body. When he was done, he tossed the whip aside and pulled off his wig. Breathing heavily, he approached an out of it La' Chat stroking his dick. Pre-cum dripped from the tip of his cock. He turned his victim over on her stomach and rammed himself up her asshole violently. Her eyes snapped open and her eyebrows rose, her mouth stuck wide open. Clenching his jaws,

Chet humped her faster and harder, holding her hands down. Blood and shit oozed from around her stretched out rectum, as he continued to punish her opening. He hurled all kinds of degrading insults until he was finished with her. Afterwards, he had his way with her vagina and forced her to suck him off until he relieved himself inside of her mouth. Taking the time to wipe his limp meat off on her pillow, he then pissed on her and left the basement. La'Chat lay in a fetal position in a world of hurt, sobbing. The blue illumination from the television screen flickered on her person in the darkness. She cried her eyes out until she fell asleep.

Over the next four years, Chet did this same ritual to La'Chat. Only he sat up a camcorder to film the sick acts, keeping footage and a journal of the things that he done to her. The crazy thing about it was little momma had become accustomed to his brutal and bizarre treatment of her. She knew the time he would come down into the basement and how long it would take. He never broke his routine. At times, La'Chat thought she was going insane being locked up and fed like some mothafucking animal and shit. She became depressed and started hearing and seeing things that weren't there. To combat these delusions, Chet had her checked out by a doctor that was into the same sick shit that he was. The mothafuckas belonged to a club of men that held the same interests: child molestation, pornography, rape and torture. The members identified themselves through the tattoos on their forearms. It was the inking of a lion's roaring head.

La'Chat would pray to God for one of his angels to come and save her. Years had passed and she never had gotten that angel. That's when she decided to kill herself. She planned to run as fast as she could across the room until the chain she was shackled to forcefully snapped her neck.

On the night that she decided to go through with her plans of suicide, someone had broken into the house. She heard elevated voices and threats being thrown around. Then there was gunfire. The shots sounded like they came from a handgun and some kind of a revolver. A .357 Magnum she assumed. Anyway, the basement door swung open and she heard a gasping Chet and his hurried footsteps. She made out the yellow light that shined on the wall of the basement and his silhouette as he ran down the steps as fast as he could. Occasionally, he would stop to open fire on whoever was chasing him. By the time he reached the basement floor and turned around to take another shot, he was already taking a hot one to the mouth and face. His blood splattered against the wall and he dropped his weapon, falling sloppily to the surface.

La' Chat's eyes grew big and she gasped, placing her hands to her mouth. She looked for some place to hide, but there wasn't any place for her to take cover. That's when she decided to face her fate whatever it may be. She stood where she was listening to the footsteps of the booted feet as they descended the steps in a hurry. With the bald headed, muscular man finally stepped down to the surface, she could have sworn she saw a halo over his head and wings on his back. She blinked twice and realized that her eyes had been playing tricks on her.

Zay checked the pulse in Chet's neck and discovered that he was dead. He was startled when he first saw La'Chat, especially with her being chained to the wall like she was inside of some fucking dungeon. Taking a look around, he figured out what homeboy had been doing with her. This angered him, and he popped another cap into his already dead body. Afterwards, he approached a frightened La'Chat. She had her eyes squeezed shut and appeared to be praying. Her ears were flooded with the sound of Zay's boots against the cement floor. His shadow eclipsed her as he advanced in her direction. As soon as he grabbed her by her neck shackle, she tensed and prayed harder, tears jetting down her cheeks.

"Hold still, lil' momma," he told a sixteen year old La' Chat. Using the butt of his .357 Magnum revolver, he beat the pad-lock from off of the metal loop in the shackle. The broken pad-lock dropped to the floor and he removed the shackle,

dropping it as well. La'Chat backed away from him, a line creasing her forehead. She looked upon him like she couldn't believe that he didn't try to harm her.

"Why...why did you save me?" she asked, tears pouring down her face in buckets.

He opened his mouth to reply and she jumped into his arms, holding him tightly. She kissed him on the cheek and thanked him. Right after, her entire form trembled and she broke down in his arms, sobbing. Hesitantly, he embraced her and told her that everything was going to be all right. He then broke their tender moment and held her at arm's length, looking into her sadden eyes. She wiped them with the back of her hand as she listened to him speak.

"Lil' momma, do you know where this mothafucka's stash is?" Still wiping her eyes, she nodded yes. "Where? Tell me where it's at?" La'Chat pointed behind Zay and he looked over his shoulder. Hurriedly, he approached the furnace and opened its door. Inside, he found a duffle bag halfway filled with stacks of money. The muscle head nigga smiled and licked his chops, seeing he had a nice score. He then zipped up the duffle bag and slung it over his shoulder, stepping back to La' Chat. "Look, you free to go, I'ma gone and get outta here before The Ones show up, okay?" he didn't wait for her response, he tucked his revolver on his waistline and made for

the staircase. He was about to head upstairs, but she called him back. "What's up?"

"Let me come with you, please." La'Chat asked with her hands together. She didn't know where he was going, but she knew she wanted to be with him. Shit, she never wanted to be alone ever again if she could help it.

"Lil' momma, the life I lead is a fast and dangerous one." He told her truthfully. "Trust me when I say you don't want any parts of what my lifestyle has to offer." Having said that, he grasped the guardrail and planted his foot on the step. He was about to begin his climb up the staircase, but her calling out to him again stopped him.

"I'll clean, iron and cook for you."

He stopped and turned around, angling his head to the side. "You can cook?"

"Well..." she looked off to the side and then back to him. "I can't cook, but if you let me come with you I'll learn. I'll learn and I'll cook for you every day. Whatever you want, I swear to God." She looked at him pleadingly and waited to hear what his response would be. He looked off to the side, massaging his chin. Coming up with his answer, he let his hand drop to his side and said, "Okay. You can come along, but you do what I say when I say it. And no back talk." He stated firmly, wagging his finger at her and giving her a stern

look. The look in his eyes said he wasn't up for any bullshit and that he'd get rid of her ass if she didn't mind him.

She nodded and said, "Okay. You're the boss."

He sat his duffle bag down on the floor and removed his trench coat, revealing the thermal that he had on underneath it. The outlining of his Kevlar bulletproof vest shone through the thick fabric. Zay draped his coat over La'Chat's bikini clad body, picked the duffle bag up and nudged her to follow him up the staircase.

"All right then, come on." He threw his head towards the door of the basement.

La'Chat shacked up with Zay. She did exactly like she said she would do for him, and he appreciated it all. She became inquisitive of what he did for a living and begged him to show her the tricks of the trade. He did. From there on, their bond grew into a beautiful relationship. Not only did they become lovers and friends, but crime partners as well. They fell madly in love, but Zay refused to have sex with her until she was eighteen. It had been two years since she had sex, so she felt just like a virgin. She cried their first time together. It was romantic and passionate. And even to this day she considers him her first everything, regardless of what had taken place between her and Chet.

Present

Although La'Chat was ecstatic about being pregnant, she had to be real with herself. She and Zay were going to get the death penalty for putting the smash down on that D.E.A agent. With both of them gone, their child would grow up in foster care and most likely be subjected to the street life. At least that's what she believed. Realizing that this was quite possibly her baby's future, her eyes misted with tears and she shut her eyelids, sending tears flying down her cheeks. She climbed into bed and lay on her side in a fetal position, hugging herself. Her shoulders shuddered and the tears flowed uncontrollably. When she woke up everything will have been a nightmare. She and Zay would be a couple of squares working office jobs and raising their child. As this beautiful fairytale manifested in her brain, she drifted off to a peaceful sleep wearing a smile across her face.

***

When Victoria awoke there wasn't a part of her that wasn't hurting, especially her pussy. It felt like it had been ripped in half. She reached down between her legs and her palm came away slick with blood and semen. She winced when she done this because the slightest touch below brought a blinding pain to her. Her eyes welled up with tears almost instantly. A foul stench came across her nasal passages. She tilted her head back and inhaled deeply. The air smelled of sex and blood. This made her want to vomit, but she held fast to her dinner. There was dry and wet semen on her back, and her face was swollen from being struck with the butt of one of the henchmen's AK-47s. Sliding her tongue around inside of her mouth, she came across something with a slimy texture that tasted like garbage. She hawked it up to the front of her throat and spat it out. Looking down, she saw that it was semen. Seeing this disgusted her. She heaved and heaved until she threw up the contents of her stomach, splattering the surface below her.

Victoria scanned the floor for an area that wasn't covered with semen and blood. Finding it near the corner of the basement, she crawled over to it like a baby and laid down in a fetal position. It was then that she took a deep breath and shut her eyelids. Finally, she could do what she wanted to do during her rape, she broke down bawling. Her body shuddered and her nostrils flared as her tears slid down her face, dripping onto the floor creating small puddles.

Flashback

Victoria sat a glass down beside hers and picked up the bottle of Brandy. "Have a drink with me." She said to Ren. Before he'd answered she was filling two glasses. She picked up her glass and he picked up his glass. "Salute," They clinked their glasses together and took a sip. The telephone rang and she snatched it up. "Hello! Jail? What happened? OK. I'll send someone to make the…"

Boom!

An explosion rocked the mansion with the strength of an earthquake.

"What the hell was that?" Ren shot to his feet and drew his banger, ready to give a bitch ass nigga a tombstone.

Victoria looked to the security screen on her desk and saw a drove of men carrying machineguns spilling through the doorway of her mansion. Once her eyes sent the information to her brain what was happening, her heart thundered inside of her chest. Her eyes bulged and she gasped.

"Shit! We're under attack!" Victoria dropped the telephone to the floor and grabbed her cell phone. Afterwards, she called the only person that she could think of. They didn't pick up so she left them a message. Next, she unzipped her jeans and stuffed it inside of her pussy. She rushed over to her book shelf and pulled on a thick burgundy book. Something clicked and the opposite side of the shelf slid back. A few Kevlar bulletproof vests and an arsenal of weapons were exposed. She grabbed two bulletproof vests, strapping one to her body and throwing one to Ren. Next, she then snatched up two AK-47s with drums, keeping one for herself and tossing one over to Ren. At the same time they checked the banana

clips then smacked them back in, cocking the hammers on their deadly weapons and heading for the door. Ren reached for the door-knob.

Boom!

The door was blown off by an explosion, fire and black smoke filled the study. Victoria lay on her back gagging and coughing on smoke while Ren lay under the door. He was missing an arm and his left leg had been stripped down to the bone. They both narrowed their eyes into slits trying to see through the smoke and debris. The smoke cleared revealing the man behind all of the mayhem. He was a brown skinned man of average height with a protruding gut. He had a nest of dark hair and thick a beard. The hair on his face made him look wolf like. The shades that he was wearing showed the fires that were scattering throughout the study's floor.

The brown skinned man lumbered forth wearing a cast and clutching an M-16. The further he walked into the study the more of him came into view until all of him was shown. He smiled wickedly and his evil eyes bore into Victoria's. She gritted her teeth and then spat at his boots.

"Diablo." she spoke his name.

Seeing Diablo moving in on his boss, Ren reached for his AK-47 with his one good hand. Even as a cripple he was going to give his all to save his boss's life, it was his duty. He wrapped his hand around the handle of the choppa and swung it around.

Blaaaaaaaaaaaaaaaaaaaat!

Diablo walked past Ren. Without even looking, he pointed his M-16 at him and pulled the trigger. The missile shaped bullets blew Ren's face off, stripping it down to the bloody skeletal bone structure of his skull. Diablo's henchmen poured inside of the study and surrounded Victoria. At Diablo's orders they snatched Victoria up by her arms and held her up against the wall. She mad dogged Diablo with a viciousness that would cause you to think that she'd bare her teeth and tear his throat out of his neck.

"I see you gotta lotta fire in you, I like a feisty bitch, I'm gonna have fun extinguishing them flames." He smiled and licked his chops, grabbing the bulge in his jeans suggestively.

"Fuck you, puto!" she hawked up phlegm and spit in his face. The nasty goo splattered against his forehead and dripped from off of his brow. He wiped it off and sucked it from off of his fingers, smiling at her devilishly. "You try to bring anything near my mouth and I'll bite it the fuck off!" she growled like a lioness defending its cub, spittle flying every-where.

"Oh yeah?"

"Yeah, mothafucka!"

"How about this?" Diablo pointed his M-16 at Victoria's forehead. She didn't bat an eyelash. Nah, her face twisted in hatred and she gritted. The drug lord held his deadly weapon on her for a while. Then he suddenly, whipped it by her ear, and pulled the trigger. Fire spat out of the assault rifle, as it rang out loud and furiously. The elevated noise set off an eerie siren in the queen pin's ear. Her eyelids snapped opened and her lips peeled apart. Her head bobbled about and she blinked her eyes repeatedly. She went limp in Diablo's henchmen's arms, hanging like a rag doll. "Tie this cunt's wrists and ankles and throw her into the back of the van." He gave the order to his henchmen and then looked to two others. "Keno and Chuncho, follow me. We're gonna burn this hen house down." With that said, the henchmen went on to carry out their boss's commands.

Diablo and his henchmen came down the stairs of the mansion, slinging their assault rifles over their shoulders. They followed their boss into the dining room, where they held him kick over the white grand piano. He ordered them to pull down the curtains and tear them into strips, while he kicked the legs off of the piano. Once he was done, he tossed the henchmen their individual legs and had them wrapped the strips around the ends of them, like he did. Afterwards, he whipped out his Zippo lighter and threw it open. Having given birth to a flame, he used it to ignite the strips that were tied around the ends of their piano legs as well as his. Toting the homemade torches, they went around the mansion. They kicked over furniture and set fire to it. Once they were done with the furniture, they set fire to the curtains inside of all of the bedrooms. It wasn't long before Victoria's home was a burning inferno that had everyone hot and sweaty.

"Lemme go, lemme go, you bastards!" Diablo heard Victoria's voice from above. He looked up and saw her struggling to get away from his men. She kicked one of them in the nuts and doubled him over. The other, she threw her head back, busting his nose. He staggered backwards, blood flooding down the lower half of his face. With the henchmen distracted, Victoria took off running down the staircase, wrists bound behind her. She was so focused on the men that she'd attacked, that she didn't realize that she was running down the stairs where Diablo was. When she turned around and saw him smiling devilishly again, her eye lit up and she gasped. She ended up tripping and tumbling down the steps, sliding on the waxed floor. She lay on her side wincing and peering up through narrowed eyelids. Before she knew it, Diablo grabbed her by the neck and pulled her up to her feet. Staring her dead in her eyes, he gave her a squeezed that caused her to gag and a vein to pulsate at her temple.

"Now, where did you think you were going?" Diablo released her and then whacked her upside the head with his cast. She spun around and hit the floor, dizzy. Standing where he was, he watched as his men came down stairs and snatched her up. One of them threw her over his shoulder and carried her out of the burning mansion. Diablo and the rest of the men followed. They got into two separate vans. The one that the drug lord was in was the first to slide the door shut and drive off. The last van's sliding door was slid open by the man that had Victoria thrown over his shoulder. She lay where she was, looking at her burning mansion. The golden flames of the fire illuminated her face and she saw the flaming residence in both of her pupils. Tears pooled in her eyes and ran down her cheeks hastily. She wasn't sad about losing the mansion. Nah, she could purchase another with all of the money she had. What she was emotional about was Ren being killed and his body being left to burn to ashes.

The man took Victoria from over his shoulder and threw her inside of the van. Next, he climbed inside and slid the door shut. Afterwards, he pulled a black pillowcase over her head so that she wouldn't know where she was being taken. Using the butt of his AK-47, he stomped the floor. At that moment, the driver of the van drove off.

Present

Wiping her face with the side of her arm, Victoria sniffled and sat upright. She opened her legs like she was going to give birth to a baby. Her face slightly twitched as she made her pussy contract, slowly working the cell phone out that she'd shoved inside of herself. Before she knew it, the cellular dropped out onto the floor. She picked it up and looked at its screen. The battery was dead, but that wouldn't stop someone from trying to find her. She could still be located.

See, Victoria's cellular had a GPS app, which was linked to Lafayette, Gar and Lil Man's cell phones. She'd done this in case she found herself in a situation, like the one that she was in now. Now, she knew that Lafayette wasn't going to come rescue her, because he was locked up. So her fate rested in the hands of Gar. Although Lafayette would bust his gun, his right-hand man was a coldblooded killa. She knew that Diablo had control over a small army, so she only hoped that the thug would come rolling out with a cavalry of his own.

Chapter Six

Knock! Knock! Knock! Knock!

Gar rapped on the thick wood door and looked over his shoulders, making sure no one was trying to creep up on him. Seeing that there wasn't anyone trying to do him any harm, he looked down at his ruined leg and grimaced. The mothafucka felt like it was on fire. He couldn't wait to get inside of the house and get whatever pain killas his mother may have for him.

Gar looked alive hearing the locks coming undone and the chain being taken off of the door. The door was pulled open and light cut into the darken porch, lighting him up. He stood face to face with his mother, Lacey. Lacey was a petite woman that stood an even five feet. She had short hair, which was feathered at its ends and skin the color of almonds. There was a very large mole above her top lip, that couldn't help drawing anyone that looked in her direction attention. At the moment, she was dressed in a dark gray turtle neck, jeans and boots.

One look at Lacey and you would never think that she was once a crackhead, but it was indeed true. In fact, her lifestyle had nearly cost her, her life.

Flashback

When Gar's father died of a heart attack his mother turned to smoking crack to deal with his passing. Her priorities went out of the window and she winded up losing her job and their house. From there, they were living in abandoned houses and rustling up food where ever they could. Gar was breaking bad in the streets robbing, scamming, and petty hustling trying to get by. The young nigga was raising his self while his momma, Lacey, was selling her pussy and stealing to support her habit. However, once her looks had faded, and none of the D-boys wanted to fuck her, she just stuck to finessing niggaz out of their drugs. Well, one day, she made the mistake of stealing this local small time nigga'z product by the name of Bash. Homie was mad as shit and he wanted to tax that ass badly for the violation. He paid Lacey's smoking partner off with some rocks for her whereabouts and they gave up her current location.

Bash didn't waste any time tying a black bandana around the lower half of his face and grabbing a baseball bat from out of the trunk of his car. He came through the broken out window at the back of the house that a black garbage bag was taped over. He tore the garbage bag free and climbed inside, stepping down into the sink as quietly as he could. Looking up, he found Lacey in the living room smoking crack. Gripping the baseball bat with both hands, he snuck up on that ass and brought his bat down on her shoulder. She dropped her crack pipe; it deflected off the tip of her raggedy sneaker and rolled across the hardwood floor. Throwing her head back, she screamed so loud that she went hoarse and tears welled up in her eyes. Bash struck her back and she spun around, throwing up her arm to defend herself. Seeing that she was wide open, he swung the bat into her stomach will all the might he could muster. She howled in pain and went stumbling backwards, falling through a glass coffee-table. The table exploded and sent shards flying everywhere. Lacey lay on her back whimpering and holding her arm.

Bash pulled the bandana down from the lower half of his face and said, "Now, I know yo' ol' smoked out ass didn't think you was gone steal from me without some penalties and fees, did ya?" he scowled and kicked her in the stomach so hard that she slightly lifted off of the floor, face twisted in into a mask of hurt. Her eyes snapped open and she gasped for air, using her good arm to hold her stomach. "Uh huh, shit hurt, don't it? Now, the arm that you use to steal from me was the penalty, but yo' life? That's gone be the fee, bitch!" he lifted his baseball bat over his head and snarled, menacing eyes casted down on her.

"Oh please, God, no! I'm sorry, Bash!" Lacey sobbed and pleaded. She threw up her arm and leg to shield her from his assault.

"Fuck a sorry, hoe!" he spat and swung the baseball bat downward.

POP!

Bash's eyes grew big and he dropped the baseball bat. It chattered when it hit the floor and rolled to a stop. He looked over his shoulder and found Gar pointing a smoking snub nose .38 sideways at him, like they do in hood movies. Bash's face tightened with anger and he charged the young nigga growling. Gar squeezed off rapidly, hand slightly jerking. The chamber of the pistol twisted with every shot that its barrel released.

POP! POP! POP! POP! POP!

The youth squeezed the trigger of the pistol until the chamber clicked empty. Seeing that he had dropped Bash dead, he ran over to his mother. He pulled her to her feet and she wrapped her arms around him. She kissed him at the top of his head and rubbed her hand up and down his back, staring down at her deceased drug dealer. Tears spilled down her cheeks. This wasn't because that bastard with the holes in him was dead. Nah, her tears were because her stealing had lead to her son staining his soul forever by taking a life.

Gar and his mother cleaned up all of the evidence and rolled Bash up in a floor rug. They took him into the backyard and buried him six feet inside of the dirt. The killing of Bash did little to affect Gar, but the same couldn't be said for his mother. She was haunted by nightmares of the deed, which lead her to smoking more crack. It wasn't until one night that she'd gotten shot by a liquor store clerk and was left bleeding inside of an alley that she vowed to change her life. An image of her Lord and Savior appeared before her very eyes, shining like a lantern. The image didn't say anything. It just stood there glowing and staring at her. After a while, Lacey shut her eyes and broke down crying and praying. It was from this occurrence that Lacey went on to check into rehab and get clean. She turned her life over to God and took a job as a counselor, helping other people get off of drugs. Her and Gar never spoke about what happened that night that he'd murdered Bash and they'd buried him. It was a secret between them that they'd take to their graves.

Present

Lacey smiled when she laid eyes on Gar but when she looked down and saw his leg that expression disappeared from off of her face.

Lacey stepped closer to her son and placed a hand on his waist, looking down at his broken limb. "My God, Clarence, what happened to you? Oh my goodness, and you've been shot?" her brows creased, as she took stock of his wounds. They were bleeding through the bandages that were wrapped around him.

"Momma, you got some pain killas fa me?" Gar winced, placing his hand on his mother's shoulder and checking his surroundings once again.

"Yeah, come on in." she pulled his arm around her shoulders and helped him inside of her house over the threshold. She shut the door behind him and locked all of the locks on it and then helped him over to the couch, lying him down. "I'll be right back with those pills." She said and headed down the hallway.

Gar lie on the couch taking in his mother's living room. It had a sectional sofa and an ottoman. They both were brown leather and suede. There was a "32 inch flat-screen television, which sat on a stained wooden entertainment center. A large Vanilla scented candle sat on either side of the flat-screen. Over the fireplace, which was currently burning logs, was a portrait of a young Gar, Lacey and his father. On each wall there was either a religious picture or some well known framed Bible quote.

Gar nodded his head, thinking back to how much his mother had changed. When he was a young nigga block hugging and thugging, he thought his mom's would never try to get off of crack and get herself together, but she had really surprised him. She did a complete 180 degree turn. Although he wasn't big on religion, he believed The Word must have been very powerful to convert someone like his mother.

"Here you go." Lacey came from out of the kitchen with a glass of water and two pain killas. Gar was so busy taking in the décor of her house that he didn't even notice her come out of her bedroom and enter the kitchen.

"Thank you, momma," He took the pills and the glass of water. He threw the pain killas back and took a sip of water to wash them down.

Lacey frowned when she took in his attire; he was still wearing a hospital gown. It tripped her out that she hadn't noticed when she opened the door for him. "You were in the hospital?" he nodded yes. "You've been missing for a few days. I called every hospital listed and the precincts. No one had any listing of a Clarence Spivey."

"Jack Spades." He gave her a name.

"Jack Spades?" her forehead creased.

"That's my alias. La musta checked me in under that." At the mention of his homeboy's name, sadness crossed his mother's face and she bowed her head. "Something wrong, ma?" he questioned with concern.

She looked up and cracked a weak smile. "Everything is fine, baby. I bowed my head to thank the Lord for bringing you home to me."

"Oh." He sat the empty glass down on the coffee table.

"What happened for you to be hospitalized? And don't lie to me. You know I know when you're lying, your left eye twitches." She wagged her finger at him.

"You're right. I ain't lied to you since I was nine years old, I'ma grown man now. I'ma tell you everything, straight up."

"Hold on. I wanna get a get the first-aid kit to patch up this leg of yours and make you up a splint." She kissed his forehead and went to go get the first-aid kit from underneath the bathroom sink. While she was gone, Gar whipped out his gun and sat it on the coffee table. He stared at it. He knew it was in his best interest to get rid of the goddamn thing because it had that nigga Biggie's body on it. If he was to ever get caught with it then he'd be washed up, especially with his record. Still, a lifetime behind bars was something that he was ready to risk to keep his life. The blazer was the only weapon in his possession that he had to protect himself, so he was going to keep it by his side.

Lacey returned to the living room with the first-aid kit and some items to make her son a split with. She sat down on the couch, propping his leg upon a pillow that she sat on her lap.

He grimaced with each movement of his limb, it was that painful and the pain killas hadn't kicked in yet.

"Grrrrr." Gar laid his foot on top of the sofa's pillow.

Lacey removed the items from the kit that she'd need to patch up her only son's wound. She looked back and forth between him and his leg; as she went on to handle the task in mind.

"All right, Clarence, tell momma all about the little situation you're in."

Gar took a deep breath and told his mother how everything from beginning to now. Now, most niggaz wouldn't have told their loved ones their business because should the law ever catch up to them they could what their family knew against them. This was true for most, but Gar love and trusted his mother. Besides that, they caught a body together so he knew that she'd keep what he was telling her between them.

"Outta of the frying pan and into the fire," She said, having heard the last of her son's story.

"Yep, outta the frying pan and into the fire." He replied, picking up the glass of Hennessy his mother had poured him up during the telling of his story and taking another casual sip from it. Afterwards, he sat the glass down on the ottoman and watched his mother put the homemade splint on him, "Thanks, ma."

"Don't mention it, son." She rubbed his thigh and then patted it.

"Where's junior?" he asked.

"He's asleep in the other bedroom."

"Good. I'ma go see 'em."

"All right."

"Grrrrr." Gar clenched his jaws and his nostrils flared, struggling to get up from off of the sofa. Seeing her son straining, Lacey got to her feet and helped him up. She then passed him the crutch she'd found in the back of the closet. He took it and placed it under his arm, using it to head towards the hallway. He was making his way towards the guest bedroom where Little Gar was residing.

"Aye," his mother called after him.

He stopped and turned around on his good leg. "Yeah, momma?" he raised his eyebrows.

"You want me to make you something to eat?"

"Nah, I'm good, momma. You still have those old pair of jeans and trench coat that I left here?"

"Yeah," She nodded. "I found some guns and a vest you left in the attic, too. The exterminator discovered them when he came to spray for termites."

"Good. I'ma need all of that. Will you be a doll and get 'em for me, ma?"

"Yes, son."

Lacey stood there lost in her son's eyes. She knew what he had in mind; he didn't have to tell her. He planned on bringing it to the bastard that shot at him and banged up his leg. She thought about reasoning with him, telling him to leave it in God's hands, but she acknowledged that he would never do that. Her son was a street nigga, and the fool that had done him up would answer to him…not the Lord.

"All right, Clarence," she nodded and watched him walk away until she disappeared. She then looked up at the ceiling, speaking to The Almighty. "Please, Father, cloak my wayward son in your blood and protect him."

Gar limped down the hallway with the supporting of his crutch. The pain killas had kicked in and he didn't feel much of his wounds, which he was thankful for. Being virtually free from the pain released him from the throngs of pain and allowed him to think clearly. Gar stopped at the bedroom next to his mother's and grasped door's knob. He twisted it and pushed the door open, making his way inside. The first thing he saw was a lump beneath a sheet, rising and falling. Instantly, he knew that it was his son breathing and peacefully sleeping. A smile stretched across his lips, he stood where he was and admired the small person that he and Batice had created. Suddenly, the smile disappeared from his face. This was because he thought about his baby momma, and the night he mothered her to death at the hospital. As much as he loved her scandalous ass, he loved his son even more and she wasn't doing right by him. She had him around crackheads and had almost gotten him killed with her bullshit in the streets. He didn't regret sending her to her Maker; he figured he was doing what was best for his son. Still, it was because of his decision that Little Gar would grow up without his mother and with the way he was living, his father as well. With neither of them around, he felt like his offspring was poised to be just like him, a product of his environment.

Pushing those thoughts to the back of his brain, Gar made his way over to his son and sat down on the bed beside him. Wincing, he leaned over and placed his ear to his back, listening to his heart beat. He smirked when he heard the undeniable rhythm of the most important muscle of his mini me's body. Bringing his head back up, he caressed his baby boy's back and talked to him.

"Hey there, Lil' G, daddy missed you. I just got outta the hospital. Well, I'ma keep it one hunnit witchu, I just fled from the 'spital. Yeah, daddy got into a shootout with a couple of bitch-boys. One of them I know, his name's Loon, which fits him, 'cause you've gotta be a crazy mothafucka to bear arms with a nigga as cold as ya daddy..." Gar's eyebrows arched and his nose scrunched up. The thought of a band of niggaz trying to take him out, pissed him the fuck off.

Them mothafuckaz wasn't stupid though. Nah, they came at a capital G while he was at his weakest. That's a kill that can't be respected, at least by me it can't. Ol' bitch ass niggaz, that's okay, 'cause they got some hot shit coming their way, straight up.

Gar focused his attention back on his son. He then went on to tell him the events that lead up to his leg getting injured. Lastly, he told him that he killed his mother and asked that he find it somehow in his heart to forgive him. His eyes built up with tears and his bottom lip trembled. He shut his eyelids and water jetted down his cheeks. Sniffling, he wiped his face with the back of his hand. "I love you, son, be safe and be strong out in these streets should you choose the life that I have." He leaned over and kissed the little nigga on his cheek. He heard the telephone ringing as he got to his good foot, planting the crutch under his arm. He had just made it inside of the living room to find his mother lying down the items he requested on the couch.

"Thank you, momma." He kissed her cheek and approvingly looked at the items he asked her to retrieve. She turned to him and gave him a halfhearted smile; he frowned seeing the sadness in her eyes. "What's wrong?" he asked, placing his hand on her shoulder.

"There's something that I meant to tell you when you came in," she stated, taking his hand into her own, caressing it.

"What is it?" he wondered, lines creasing his forehead.

"I gotta call a few days ago saying that Lafayette had been killed in the County jail." As soon as she delivered the news, tears raced down her cheeks. She wanted to tell him when she let him inside of the house, but she wasn't sure of how to break the bad news to him.

Gar stared off into space, tears building up in his eyes and lips slightly trembling. Squeezing his eyelids shut for a moment, he swallowed the ball of hurt that formed in his throat. When he peeled his eyelids back open, his eyes were just glassy. He fought back the overwhelming emotions that overcame him, not wanting to fall apart in front of his mother.

"What happened?"

"They don't know, baby. They found him inside of the shower room; someone had caved in his skull. The police are investigating it."

A confused expression crossed Gar's face and he looked to the floor. Then, he looked back up at his mother. "Ma, what did he get locked up for?"

"I…I don't know, son." she wiped her eyes with the sleeve of her shirt.

There was silence inside of the room, and Gar had this look on his face, like he was thinking about something, massaging his chin.

"The Sanchez Cartel," He said to himself. "Diablo musta put a price on his head when he got behind them walls, and that's what happened. I bet that's it, it's gotta be it."

Fucking Wetbacks, they gone feel the guns behind this shit, that's on everything I love.

"Ma, lemme see yo' laptop," Lacey went to go get her laptop. As she made to go passed her son, he stepped before her and wrapped his arm around her. He pressed her up against him gently, being mindful of his gunshot wounds. She held him and cried her eyes out. That nigga Lafayette and his brother, 8-Ball was like sons to her. The Myers Brothers and her son ran the streets together tough. She remembered nights that they slept over and ate dinner at her home. Sometimes when she was fucked up and needed a blast, Lafayette would bless her with a little something, something so she could get by. She knew that if Gar found out that the two would be at odds, and their brotherhood would probably end, so that really meant a lot to her that he would risk that. "That's right, ma, let it allllll out." Gar kissed his mother on top of the head and pulled her closer.

Lacey pulled away and wiped her face with the sleeves of her shirt. She then got the laptop and her son looked up his deceased homeboy's charges. Seeing what Lafayette went down for satisfied his curiosity, but he had to get down to the bottom of who murdered him. Realizing that he had to put that nigga Loon and his hitta asleep before he could breathe easy and get some answers, he decided to strap up and go looking for that ass. The last thing he wanted was that bitch ass nigga finding him first and letting a full clip off in his dome. He'd be damned if he let that fuck-nigga leave his little nigga fatherless.

***

Jason walked inside of his building on his way to the office inside of his firm. He made his way toward the elevators coming across people leaving. He gave nods and smiles to those that he knew, holding his briefcase to his side so he wouldn't hit them with it. Looking ahead, he saw that the elevator doors were going to close and it was heading upwards. Acknowledging this, he ran towards the elevator as fast as he could. His leather, hard bottom shoes clicked on the wax floor, which he could see his reflection on. The opening of the closing doors of the elevator was growing slimmer and slimmer in his line of vision. The people harbored inside of the elevator acted like they didn't even see him coming. At the last minute, he slid inside of the elevator breathing huskily and adjusting the cufflinks of his suit. His fall balled up and he looked around at all of the people surrounding him.

"Fuck all of you; I know you saw me coming." He pressed the button of the floor he wanted and stood upright, watching the numbers above the double doors lighting up one by one. Once his floor was reached, he watched the doors open and walked out, strolling down the corridor. He walked past his secretary and greeted her. "Good morning, Stephanie. How're you?"

"I'm fine, sir. I have a couple messages that were left for you." She said smiling, picking up the slips of papers with the messages on them and passing them to him. He thanked her and made his way towards his office, reading over the messages. Once he got to the double doors of his enormous office, he turned the gold handle and entered. He came into a spacious room with a high ceiling. It was well lit and the ceiling to floor window gave a picturesque view of the city that you could only get from a helicopter.

Jason sat his briefcase down at his desk and removed his suit's jacket, loosening his collar. He then held down the button on the intercom and told Stephanie what he wanted for breakfast, coffee included. Afterwards, he sat down in his executive chair. Scooting closer to the desk he saw the portrait of him and Montrice. His eyebrows dipped and he snatched the portrait up, grabbing the waste basket as well. He dropped the portrait inside of the waste basket and spit on the glass of it, watching it slide down. Hearing his cellular ring, he picked it up and looked at the screen. He frowned not knowing who it was, but his curiosity got the best of him so he answered it.

"Hello?" Jason spoke into the cell phone, propping his crocodile leather shoes on the desk top. Suddenly, a smile broadened across his face, mood lightening. "Heyyy, baby." He said sweetly into the receiver. The person that had called him had always been a good friend of his. They wanted to explore a relationship with him, but he couldn't bring himself to have an affair on his wife. As soon as he found out that she was cheating, he wished he'd fucked around on her. Anyway, the person he was on the phone with had recently won him over and they had been talking a lot more lately over the phone. Everything was beautiful between them, but the last thing Jason wanted was to jump into another relationship, especially after the murder of his wife. This was why they agreed to take things slow. "I'm okay. What's wrong?" he sat up in his chair, frowning up. "Sure, what kind of favor do you need? It's a tall order, but I'm sure the people I know can have it filled. Hold on." He cradled the cellular to his ear with his shoulder and grabbed a tablet and ink-pen. Listening to what he was being told, he jotted down the request. "Okay. I got it. Call me back in a couple of hours and I will let you know what the deal is. All right, I love you, too." He disconnected the call.

***

Gar hobbled into the bathroom and leaned his crutch up against the wall. Placing his hand on the porcelain sink, he hobbled over to the tub and reached for the dial. The dials squealed as they were turned. Steam flourished in the bathroom as the showerhead sprayed hot water, fogging up the medicine cabinet's mirror. Gar placed his hand into the spray of water to test its temperature, water running down his arm. It was just right. He let his towel drop to the floor before stepping into the tub, in the way of the water. He grabbed the Dove bar soap and began lathering his body with it, hot liquid coating his form. He closed his eyes and relaxed his muscles, allowing the water to ease his tension. Visions of a nude Batice played out in his head like a film. She had her thighs spread wide open and was playing with her juicy pussy, licking her lips as she stared at him lustfully. The soft moans she made caused his dick to grow to its full potential, sudsy water dripping from off the tip of it. Before he knew it, he'd dropped the bar of soap and wrapped his fingers around his meat. Licking his lips, he stroked his grown man, imagining himself balls deep inside of her. He was staring at her face to face, giving it to her hard, rough and nasty, like he always had.

"Uh! Uh! Uh! Uh!" she hollered out, head tilted back and arms wrapped around his shoulders. He had her up against the wall, and her legs were wrapped around his waist. Homie was pounding her the fuck out, grunting as he did so. Beads of sweat oozed out of his pores and some of them ran down his hot body, sliding between the crack of his hairy buttocks.

"Ahhh, shit, I'm 'bouta cum!" Gar announced, still lapping at her middle. His pelvis slapped up against her, causing her breasts to jiggle. His hot sweat splashed on her face and chest, but he kept at it.

"Gar!" she managed to say his name.

"Yes, baby?" his powerful thrust continued.

"Why...why did...did you kill me?"

"'Cause you almost got junior killed, oh, shit, I'ma 'bouta nut!"

"I know. And I'm...uh! Uh! Uh! Uh! Sorrrrryyy."

"It's too late for all of that now, lil' momma, just take this dick!"

"Baby."

"Yeah, damn, a nigga 'bouta bust."

"Look at me."

"Huh?"

"Look at me." Gar looked up at Batice. His eyes widen and he gasped, seeing the zombie version of her before him. She tilted her head and glared up at him, smiling wickedly. "You're gonna be joining me soon."

"Haa," Gar snapped out of his trance and looked alive, head darting all around the bathroom. He looked down and found his bar of soap lying by the drain. He looked to his left and found his leg in the homemade splint that his mother had created for him. Afterwards, he placed his hands on the tiled wall and breathed hard, water cascading over his body. Water circled his face and flowed in a steady stream from off of his chin. It also dripped from off of his brows and outstretched arm.

Knock! Knock! Knock! Knock!

"Clarence!"

Knock! Knock! Knock! Knock!

"Clarence!"

Gar pulled his face away from the spray of hot liquid. He swiped the excess water from off of his face and looked to the bathroom door. He took a deep breath and said, "Yeah, ma?"

"Are you all right in there? I heard you holler? Did you fall?"

"Nah, I'm fine. I'm finna get out now." he answered, twisting the dials to turn them off.

Gar hopped out of the tub and dried off.

Chapter Seven

The next morning

Jason made his way through the noisy visiting room in his expensive suit, toting a brief case. His head was on a swivel as he looked around for his client. When he spotted him, he cleared his throat and adjusted his tie. With that out of the way, he made hurried steps in his direction, giving whomever he passed en route a nod of acknowledgement. Once he finally made it to the window where his client was sitting, he sat down and sat his briefcase down beside his foot. Picking up the telephone, he rubbed it off on his suit and brought the phone to his ear. He sat there until his client finally decided to pick up his telephone. Once he reluctantly did so, they engaged in their conversation.

"How are you doing today, Mr. Curtis?" Jason began.

"I'm all right. Just give it to me straight, no chase. What're these crackas talking about, homes?"

"Okay." He took a deep breath. "They're talking about giving you and La'Chat the death penalty for murdering that agent."

There was silence as Zay stared at him. He didn't blink and make any sudden movements. He was as still as a manne-quin.

Zay finally blinked and swallowed the spit that had accu-mulated in his throat. "This is the life I chose, so I knew this moment would someday arrive. Shiiiiiit, with all of the dirt that I done did, I'd be a fool to expect me and my mine ride off into the sunset. I can bite the bullet, while looking the shooter square in his eyes...but La'Chat....the love of my life...my mothafucking heartbeat...I can't let her go out like that."

"I'm glad you said that, because there's something else I need to tell you."

"Speak on it, counselor."

"Your wife is pregnant."

A shocked expression came over Zay's face and his mouth fell open, staring at his attorney. Suddenly, he dropped the telephone. It banged off of the table and hung loosely, swing-ing back and forth. He bowed his head and massaged the bridge of his nose, taking a deep breath. Having gathered his composure, he picked the telephone back up and brought it to his ear.

"Are you, okay?" a concerned expression came across his face.

Zay nodded and went on to say what he had in mind. "Listen up; I got some information that can help me in this case. I'm talking about some information that these crackas are gonna be reallll interested in, ya feel me? Here's the catch though, homes, I'm not coming off of nothing unless they agree to let my lady walk. You hear me? Unless they talking about my lady walking up outta that shit-hole that she's in, I'ma sit on this shit." He cleared his throat with his fist to his mouth and listened to what was being said to him. "All right, well, you set the meeting up. Once we seal the deal, I wanna see La'Chat, man. I gotta touch her skin, see her face, and smell her scent. I'ma die if I never get to be in her presence again, ya feel me? I'ma die way before these crackas gas my ass."

"I'll get right on it." Jason replied.

"Appreciate it, black man. We'll chop it later."

"I'll be in touch."

The men hung up their respective phones and went on about their business.

***

The body bags were loaded into the back of the van and the double doors were slammed shut. The driver of the transporting vehicle smacked the imaginary dirt from off of his palms and made his way around the van, jumping in behind the wheel. He cranked up the vehicle and threw it into drive, mashing the gas pedal. The van drove off and emerged from the sliding barbed wire gate of the County jail. Coming out of the correctional facility, the driver turned on the turning signal and made a left. He turned on the radio and searched the channels until he found the song that he desired. As soon as he heard his favorite song, he broke out singing the lyrics of it right along with its crooner. Homie threw his head back and sung with all of the soul that his body possessed, snapping his fingers. Once he came to a red stop-light, he nodded his head and drummed his fingers on the steering wheel. He was really feeling himself. So much so that he was drawing the attention of the drivers of other cars in traffic. Looking over to his left, he saw a white woman with short her staring at him, he winked and blew her a kiss. Quickly, she snapped her head back around and adjusted her rearview mirror, acting like he didn't try hitting on her. He smiled and focused his attention back on the road. Nodding his head, he tapped his fingers on the steering wheel and tapped his foot. Unbeknownst to him, a black on black Lincoln Town Car emerged from behind a Cadillac, which was on the right of him. The classy vehicle got into the same lane that he was in, idling two cars behind him. When the stop-light turned green, the transporting van drove off. Soon, the two cars behind him went their respective ways and left the Lincoln Town Car behind. The Lincoln drove a safe distance behind the van. No one could see inside of the car, because it had limousine tinted windows. The classy vehicle looked out of place out there on the streets though. There was something dangerous and spooky about it, like it was up to no good. It gave off the same aura that the old rusty van did in The Jeepers Creepers movie.

When the van came to another stop-light, the Lincoln Town Car swung out in front of it and its doors came open. Two men wearing ski-masks jumped out wearing leather jackets zipped up to their necks. Their gloved hands pointed compact Glocks with silencers on them at the driver of the van. The driver's eyes nearly jumped out of their sockets. Hurriedly, he threw the vehicle in park and threw his hands up in the air. Tilting his head back slightly, he swallowed the ball of fear that had formed inside of his throat. Terrified, he watched the masked men move in on him. The huskier one of the two of them opened the driver side door and pulled his ass up out of the van, dropping him into the street. He then pressed his steel to the back of his skull and told him not to move or he'd put a bullet into the back of dome. The driver trembled all over, lying with the side of his face mashed into the ground and holding up his hands.

"Get the keys out of the ignition and open up the back doors." The husky man ordered the slender one in a Russian accent. The slender man did as he was told and pulled the doors open. Reaching inside, he pulled out a body bag and unzipped it. Inside he found a corpse. The corpse peeled its eyelids open. When he saw the masked man standing over him, he quickly got out of it and ran to the Lincoln Town Car. As soon as he hopped into the vehicle he slammed the door shut. The slender man ran to the front passenger door and opened it. Turning around, he hollered for his partner in crime to come on. The husky man held his gun to the back of the driver of the van's head a while longer before removing it. Afterwards, he retreated back to the Lincoln and hopped in behind the wheel, peeling off from the scene.

The man that was playing dead inside of the body bag sat in the backseat rummaging through a shopping mall bag. He put on his underwear and socks that were inside of the bag. Afterwards, he put on the clothing and sneakers. They weren't his style, but fuck it; they'd due until he found something else to his liking. Having finished getting dressed, he took a second look inside of the shopping bag and found a two blocks of money sealed in plastic. Also inside of the bag was a bottle of Hennessy, the man's favorite alcohol beverage. He looked up into the rearview mirror and made eye contact with the husky man in the passenger seat. The husky fella gave him a nod, letting him know that the rest of the items were his to have.

"Thanks. I could use a drink." The man that was in the bag cracked opened the bottle of Hennessy and took it to the head. Taking a swallow, he looked out of the window and watched the scenery change. Before he knew it, he was seeing double and feeling light headed. Blinking his eyelids continuously, he looked up front to find the husky cat staring at him. He was still wearing a ski-mask, and so was his comrade.

"My friend, tell me how many fingers do you see?" he said, holding up two fingers.

"Four! No, three," he blinked some more. "Shit, I don't know. What the fuck did y'all put in this Hennessy?" he held up the bottle, looking at its contents. Suddenly, he dropped the bottle and it hit the floor, spilling some of its contents.

"It's nothing, just a sedative. You'll be okay." He pulled back the sleeve of his leather jacket and looked at his titanium watch. "You'll be waking up in about, let's say…" he tilted his head from left to right, like he was trying to make up his mind. "Twenty to twenty-five minutes."

The entire time that the Russian was talking, it sounded like a DJ Screw mix-tape to the dude that was under the influence. His eyelids became heavier and heavier until eventually, he fell over to the side snoring. Seeing that he was sound asleep, the husky Russian turned back around in his seat.

"Is he out?" the slender Russian asked, looking back and forth between his comrade and the windshield.

"Yes." he nodded.

The Russians pulled off their ski-masks. They made it to their destination and changed out of their clothing, stuffing them into black garbage bags. She placed homie that they had drugged into the trunk of the new transporting vehicle, which was a Cougar. Afterwards, they soaked the Lincoln Town Car in gasoline and struck a match, watching the car go up in flames.

The Russians drugged their capture because they didn't want him knowing the next phase of their plan. They executed the mission that they were contacted for so their job was done.

***

Zay, Jason and two correctional officers posted up in the warden's office, waiting for La'Chat. Jason tapped his leather shoe and occasionally glanced at his Rolex. When he done it this last time, the door came open and the lady they were waiting for was escorted in. The correctional officers began removing her shackles. While they were handling the task at hand, La'Chat and Zay were smiling at one another lovingly. The muscle headed brute couldn't help taking notice that his lady had put on makeup and sprayed on perfume. He could smell her from across the office. The big man would never forget that fragrance that she was wearing, it always put him under her spell. It was Bath & Body Works' Pure Paradise. He even remembered the ocean blue, see-through bottle that the fragrance came in. It was his absolute favorite.

As soon as the shackles were removed, La'Chat rushed over to Zay and hugged him affectionately. When they pulled back, she held his face and kissed him long, deep, and passionately. They then hugged again; he shut his eyelids and inhaled her intoxicated scent. Her smell was so appeasing that it made a smile spread across his face.

"Christ, I missed you, boo." She couldn't stop smiling.

"I missed you too, baby." He rubbed her chin with his thumb, looking into her eyes.

"Baby, there's something I have to tell you." She said, looking down at his hands as she held them, they were larger than her own.

"I already know, beautiful, you're carrying our seed."

When he said this, she looked back at Jason and he nodded. He was the only one that she had told when he came to come see her about her case.

"That's why I called you here today. Not only did I want to tell you what's going on, I also wanted to see you again."

"Well, what's going on? Spit it out."

He took a deep breath and looked away. Turning back around, he made sure to look her in the face.

"You're gonna walk away from this scot-free."

She chuckled and looked down for a moment. Looking back up at him, she said, "Baby, we're waste deep in some shit here. Now isn't the time to be playing."

"Does it look like I'm playing?" he gave her his most serious expression.

Her brows furrowed. "What did you do to secure that?"

"I made a deal." He told her honestly.

"A deal?" her forehead wrinkled and her nose scrunched up. "You snitched?"

"Yeah." he nodded.

"You fucking rat!" her eyes took on a hateful glare and she clenched her jaws.

Smack!

The impact of her palm threw his face in the opposite direction. She went to hit him again and he grabbed her by the wrist. "I snitched. I snitched on myself. I did it for you, for us, for the baby." He touched her stomach.

"What did you give them?" she inquired.

"I'm holding the weight on this. Like I said before, you're gonna walk." He caressed the side of her face.

"What chu give 'em?"

"Some robberies…some murders."

"Jesus," she dropped her head and looked back up at him, eyes teary. "How much time are they talking about giving you, bae?"

Zay stood there staring into her eyes. He didn't know what to say, so he hoped his eyes did it for him.

"Life?" she tilted her head and looked up at him.

He swallowed his spit and held her gaze. That's when she knew that he would be given the death sentence. She made an ugly ass face and her eyes welled up with tears. Her bottom lip shivered and she sniffled. She smacked his ass again, harder this time. Next, she kicked him in the stomach. He doubled over and she rushed him, throwing a flurry of punches. She called him all kinds of stupid, dumb mothafuckaz as tears flew from her eyes. She was trying to hurt him, so he could feel the emotional pain that he caused her in making his decision. That's why she was hitting him with all of her might. After a while he stopped trying to block her attacks, allowing her vicious blows to land.

The correctional officers made to restrain La'Chat, but their commanding officer ordered them to stand down. He did this because Zay signaled to him that he had everything under control.

"How could you, Zay? How could you?" she slowed down on her punching of him, feeling fatigue. "I'm pregnant! We're gonna have a kid together!"

"I know, baby. And that's why I did it." He rose up from where he was doubled over and grabbed her. He gave her a loving embrace and she rested the side of her face against his broad chest, crying. His lip was busted and his nose was bleeding. He could feel the area surrounding his eye beginning to swell.

Everyone present during the meeting for the deal was present inside of the room now. This included Jason.

"Baby, what am I going to do without you?" La' Chat sniffled, looking up at her man, tears constantly running.

"You're gonna raise our child. You're gonna give him, or her a betta life than either of us ever had."

"I love you, I love you so much. I don't wanna be without you…ever."

"I know, baby, but in order for our child to have a real shot out there," he threw his head towards the door. "We're gonna have to make some sacrifices. You understand?" he asked her, wiping the tear that treaded down her cheek with his thumb. With that said, she broke down crying again, burying her face into his chest. He wrapped his big, strong arms around her again, kissing the top of her head. Once it seemed like she had settled down, he broke their embrace. Tilting her chin upwards, he kissed her lips and then her forehead. He looked to the commanding officer of the correctional officers. The commanding officer tapped the face of his wrist watch, letting him know that their time was up. "We've gotta break up this lil' tender moment of ours, baby. I'll write chu soon, okay?" she nodded. He kissed her all over her face and wiped the excess wetness from her cheeks.

"Okay." She responded timidly, still in her feelings.

La'Chat gave her man a final hug before allowing the correctional officers to shackle her down. She managed to give her husband a halfhearted smile before she was escorted towards the door. Stopping short, she looked over her shoulder at Zay.

"What do you want me to name are son or daughter?"

For a time there was silence and then he replied, shrugging, "I don't know. I'll let chu know before it's time."

La' Chat nodded and allowed the officers to escort her out of the room. Zay then waited for the officers left to shackle him down so he could be escorted back to his cell. While they were putting the chains on him, Jason stepped before him, looking him directly in the eyes.

"Stay strong, black man." He extended his hand.

Zay cracked a smirk and looked down at his hand, shaking it firmly. "I will. Thank you."

Jason gave him a nod and patted him on his shoulder, taking his leave.

That night

Gar got dressed in the over sized wife beater and jeans that his mother had laid out for him. The clothing belonged to his old man. They were too big. So he had to tuck in the wife beater and buckle his belt in the last hole in it. He then grabbed a shotgun from out of the back of the closet and a .32 pistol, along with the ankle holster in was in. He had his mother strap the holster that held the small caliber weapon around his ankle. Afterwards, he threw on the old trench coat and smacked an L.A fitted cap on his crown, pulling it down low. Next, he slipped on black sunglasses and tied a black bandana around his neck. Having racked his shotgun, he turned around to face his mother. She motioned for him to bow his head and he obliged her. She unlatched the gold crucifix from around her neck and clasped it around her son. Right after, she kissed her finger tips and pressed them against the cross that dangled from the thin necklace. Next, she wrapped her arms around his neck and embraced him lovingly. He kissed her on her cheek and caressed her back.

"I guess there's nothing I can say that will get chu to change your mind about going after this Loon character, huh?" she held his hand with both of hers, looking up into his eyes. Her eyes pleaded with him to change his mind, but his facial expression showed no signs of even considering it.

"No." he shook his head. "I gotta do this. I can't put this in the Lord's hands."

"I understand." She assured him, batting her eyelashes. This action caused tears to slide down her cheeks.

Using his hand, Gar wiped the tears away that stained his mother's face and looked her square in the eyes.

"Take care of my son, ma. Raise him betta than you raised me, okay?" Lacey nodded yes. He kissed her forehead and made his way for the door. His mother turned around just in time to see the front door being shut behind her son.

Before Gar got down to the business at hand, he needed to get himself another cell phone. He went up to Sprint and copped himself another phone, getting it activated with the same telephone number as the last cellular that he had. Once the device was operational, he checked his voice messages. He was surprised when he heard Victoria's message, his forehead crinkling with lines. From what he heard it sounded like a fucking warzone taking place at her mansion. Although there was a lot of gunfire taking place, he was still able to make out the queen pin's instructions on what to do. She was going to stash her cellular phone on her person. Being that it had a GPS location device app that was directly linked to him and Lafayette's cell phones, he'd know where to find her. The way he saw it was she was hoping that he'd rally the troops and come rescue her from where ever she was being taken.

Acknowledging that Victoria was in trouble, Gar was going to put his beef with Loon behind him for the time being. He sole mission was to rescue Victoria from whatever hell that she was in. Now, he could have left her out to hang to dry, but the way he saw it homegirl saved he and Lafayette's lives. They were dead in the streets and those bricks that she saw fit to bless them with, put them back on top of the mothafucking food chain. With that mind, Gar pulled up the GPS app in his device and looked up Victoria. He smiled with satisfaction seeing exactly where she was.

"Hold on, sis, I'm on my way."

Chapter Eight

Cuba linked back up with Loon at his crib. He found himself sitting on his bed as he pulled out guns and Kevlar bulletproof vests. Loon had grabbed a shotgun and a new .32 handgun. He passed the boy Cuba one of the bulletproof vests and a Glock .50.

"Damn, my nigga, you ain't playin', is you?" Cuba looked from Loon to the bulletproof vest he was given, holding it up to his torso.

"Hell mothafucking naw," He strapped on his bulletproof vest and tucked his .32 on his waistline. "That nigga'z out there hurting. Gunshot wounds and a busted up fucking leg, homie isn't in the best of shape right now. Now, I don't know about chu, but I don't got no problems with picking a nigga off when he'd down bad. Shit, a win is a win to me, no matter how you go about getting it, ya feel me?"

"I feel you, and I'm all for getting this nigga, so don't get me wrong, but…"

"But what?" he stopped lacing up his Nike Cortez.

"But the streets is hot, hot as a mothafuckin' fire cracka. You think twelve ain't gone be out in the jungle lookin' for the niggaz that laid that down back at the 'spital? If so, you'z a mothafuckin' fool."

Loon finished lacing up his sneakers and stood up, closing the distance between him and Cuba. He cupped his hands around the young killa'z face and looked him dead in his eyes, taking a deep breath. "I hear all of that noise you making, my young nigga, but there's only one problem."

"Oh yeah? What's that?" he held his gaze and saw madness in his eyes.

Loon licked his lips and leaned closer, breathing into his face, "I. Don't. Give. A. Fuck. As of now all I care about his laying this mothafucka flat out in these streets with his brains on the curb. I cannot, and, I will not, sleep another night until that man is dead, you hear me, youngin?"

"Yeah, I hear you."

"Good," Loon cracked a smile and patted him on the cheek. He retreated to his nightstand's drawer and retrieved something.

"What chu doing, my nigga?"

"Grabbing the extra bullets for this strap before I forget them." he told him, shoving whatever he'd gotten out of the drawer into his pocket. "Come on; let's have a drink before we get back in the field."

"Alright," He nodded. Loon threw his arm over his shoulders and ushered him over to the island inside of the kitchen. He set out two glasses, which he filled with ice. Next, he took down a bottle of Hennessy and poured the glasses half full. He and Cuba then picked up their respective glasses, proposing a toast. "To loyalty…"

"To loyalty," Cuba replied. They were about to touch glasses, but Loon halted his glass. This caused Cuba's brows to crinkle.

"Hold up. We can't sip Henny with no chaser." He sat the glass down. "Yo' grab that bottle of Coke outta the frig fa me, my nigga." When Cuba turned his back and opened the refrigerator, Loon took the pill capsule from underneath his tongue and broke it over one of the glasses, releasing a powdery substance that was sure to kill whoever consumed it. Keeping his eyes on his little homie, he quickly stirred up the alcohol with his finger. By the time homeboy was turning back around, Loon was done with the task at hand.

Loon figured that now was as good as a time as any to rid himself of Cuba. He remembered what he said on their way back from the hospital about him being a known affiliate of Biggie's and the police coming to talk to him about the incident that had occurred that night. Now, Loon knew that Cuba didn't have any quarrels with busting a head. The boy was a straight up killa. What he didn't know was how he would handle himself under questioning. For all he knew the young nigga would fold faster than a lawn chair and give those boys with the badges any information that they wanted. This was a chance that Loon wasn't willing to take, so Cuba's black had to go asap.

Cuba went on to pour some of the soda into the glasses and stirred them up. Again they lifted their glasses, touching them in a toast. They were about to take a sip of their alcoholic beverages, but the house phone rang.

"Hold up. Let me answer this phone." Loon sat his glass down and headed inside of his bedroom. Cuba listened to what he said once he picked up the telephone. "Who? Nah, my nigga, you got the wrong number. Yeah, I'm sure. Don't no mothafucking Half Dead stay here. Check my attitude? Nigga, suck my dick!" he disconnected the call and walked out of the bedroom, heading for the kitchen. "Ol' bitch ass nigga." He said under his breath, like he had people around that he didn't want to hear him. Stepping back up to the island inside of the kitchen, he picked up the glass and said, "Now, where were we? Oh yeah, a toast," He lifted his glass and Cuba followed right behind him.

***

Briiiing! Briiiing! Briiiing!

His eyelids made slight movements as his eyes moved from left to right. He had slowly begun to come out of his slumber due to the ringing cell phone. His eyelids finally peeled open and he looked at his surroundings. He was inside of the basement of an old house. There were cobwebs at every corner of the walls and the window was smeared with so much dirt you couldn't see in or out. However, he could make out something moving past it. Figuring that it was a cat or dog since it had four legs; he didn't pay it any mind. Besides, that ringing cellular had homie's attention. Looking at the cell phone, a line etched across his forehead. It belonged to him.

Briiiing! Briiiing! Briiiing!

He picked up the device and looked at its screen. Unavailable was across the display. The cell phone stopped ringing and missed call appeared across the display. A second later, the ringing started back up, startling him. Again, unavailable was on the display. Curious, he slid the image of the green phone to the right and brought the device to his ear.

"Hello?" his eyes moved from left to right, listening to whoever had called him. "I'm good. I don't know…looks like I'm inside of a basement somewhere." He got to his feet and began his climb up the staircase, steps squeaking. "Yeah, I'm finna get up outta here now. Don't worry about me; I'll hit chu up when I need you. All right, bye."

He made his way across the living room of the old decrepit house, heading for the window. He peered out through the cracks of the boarded up windows and saw a dog catcher's van. At that moment, the dog catcher came running past his line of vision with the tool he used to capture hounds. He was on the tail of a straggly Doberman pinscher.

Seeing that the dog catcher was busy trying to restrain the stray hound, the man that had awoken in the basement crept out of the house. He made his way out of the yard hunched down, moving as quietly as he could. The closer he got to the man, the louder he could hear the dogs barking. It was from this he realized that they may have been hungry and agitated. Carefully, he picked up a brown beer bottle that lie abandoned on the curb and snuck upon the dog catcher. Homie had just put the stray hound inside of his vehicle, when the beer bottle exploded against the side of his skull. Glass shards with flying everywhere and alcohol slid down the back of his neck. He crumbled to the street wincing in pain, rolling from side to side. After taking the poor bastard's keys, the cat that cracked him upside his head slid in behind the wheel of his transporting vehicle. He started that big mothafucka up and drove off, leaving smoke from the exhaust pipes behind him.

***

Loon tilted the glass to take a sip of his alcohol beverage when he saw the residue from the drug he thought he emptied into Cuba's glass inside of his own. Loon held the glass at his lips and looked to Cuba. It was from this that the young killa knew that he discovered that he'd switched their glasses. Dropping their glasses at the exact same time, Loon and Cuba drew their respective guns, but the latter was slower on the draw. Cuba caught one in the shoulder and stumbled backwards, bumping into the kitchen counter and cabinets. Peeling his eyelids back open, he saw Loon about to take another shot at him, so he ran towards the living room. The entire time Loon's .32 was following right behind him like a shark in water. The young nigga moved like a bolt of lightning, head bowed and face balled up, hoping that he was fast enough to miss the bullet meant to take his life. Figuring now was the time to take the kill-shot, Loon pulled the trigger. His weapon blew back. A little before the shot echoed off the walls of the house, Cuba had dove to the floor and rolled. Coming back up, he ran to the door. He was so scared of getting shot that his hand was unsteady as he tried to remove the chain from the door. Just as he was pulling the door open, his enemy smiled satanically and pulled the trigger again. He was nauseated from the poison he'd consumed though, so the shot went wild and found a home in the door. Cuba ducked down further and ran out of the house. Loon staggered to his feet, throwing up the poison in his system. Not wanting to let his prey get away, he darted to the door and as soon as he opened it, an ember took of his ear. He howled in pain and blinked continuously, a siren blaring inside of his ear. Realizing that he was left out in the open for the young killa to pick him off, he hurried to his left and found safety behind a pillar on the porch. With his back against it and his head turned towards the street, he touched where his ear once was and his fingers came away bloody. Cautiously, he eased his head from behind the pillar so as not to get his mothafucking head blown off. As soon as the young killa saw his brows emerge, he took two more shots at him, which sent debris flying. Afterwards, he took off running down the block, occasionally glancing over his shoulder.

"Haa! Haa! Haa! Haa! Haa!" Sweat beaded on Cuba's forehead. His body was hot but his perspiration made him damp. Unbeknownst to him, Loon jumped from the porch to the bottom of the steps, hastily limping out to the sidewalk. He lifted and pointed his weapon, squeezing off rapidly. He missed his intended target. The first shot caused Cuba to run that much harder, but the second one made him zig zag, trying to avoid catching something blazing hot. "Fuck this! I ain't no mothafuckin' mark!" His eyebrows arched and he clenched his jaws, peeling his lips back in a sneer.   Stopping, he whipped around and got his tool off. His returning fire made Loon's ass duck and run as best as he could, fleeing towards the front porch.

An oncoming light illuminated Cuba's face and he narrowed his eyelids into slits. Peeling them back open, he saw twin, white orbs, which was the headlights of a Mercury Mountaineer. Quickly, he ran out into the street and pointed his blazer at the silhouette behind the wheel. Almost instantly, the SUV came to a screeching halt. Taking a glance over his shoulder, he saw Loon limping as fast as he could off of the porch again. Turning back around, he pointed his gun into the driver of the truck's face and snatched open his door. He tried yanking his ass out but for some odd reason the mothafucka wouldn't budge. Realizing that he was strapped in by the safety belt, he unbuckled it and pulled him out, letting him hit the street hard. Up the block, Loon reloaded his weapon and limped towards Cuba. By this time, police car sirens had filled the air; the combatants could hear the law coming far off in the distance.

Cuba pulled the driver side door shut and placed his blazer down on the front passenger seat. Afterwards, he shifted the behemoth into drive and mashed the gas pedal. It took off. Cuba gripped the steering wheel with both hands, one of them stained crimson. The lines of his forehead deepened and crinkles formed around his nose. He mashed the gas pedal further and further, causing the red hand of the speedometer to spin around. His vengeful eyes were focused on that nigga Loon, because he was going to mow his ho ass down.

"Let's play chicken, bitch!" Cuba said, eyes still on Loon.

"Let's play then, mothafucka!" Loon read his enemy's lips from where he stood in the street, the area where his ear was dripping blood. Lifting his weapon with both hands, he angled his head and squeezed off successively. Fire whizzed through the windshield and made cobwebs out of the glass, causing Cuba to duck down. Peering through the broken up window, he could still see the lower half of Loon's body. From the waist down he was visible, standing how he was when he'd taken his first shots. This let the young killa know that he was still attempting to pop off at him. A couple of more bullets through the windshield confirmed this. Pissed off, Cuba mashed the pedal further and accelerated the truck. It made the vehicles lined up on both sides of the street look like blurs it was racing down the residential block so goddamn fast. Still, Loon stood where he was and continued to fire. The headlights of the Mountaineer shined on the front of him, making it appear as if he was about to be abducted by an alien space craft.

"Eat shit!" Cuba hollered out to him. The Mountaineer blew past several houses so fast that debris and loose trash went into the air. The headlights of the Mercury were shining so bright that it blinded Loon. Taking note of how close he was to being run over, he dove out of the way at the last minute, feeling the air of the SUV as it blew past him. Cuba slammed on the brakes and brought his stolen truck to a screeching halt. When he looked over his shoulder and saw Loon picking up his .32 and scrambling to feet, his face tightened with anger. "Lucky fuckin' bastard," he shifted the behemoth into reverse and floored it again. Loon sent hot shit whizzing through the back window of Cuba's truck, making the window's glass implode. The young killa narrowed his eyelids into slits and ducked down, still gripping the steering wheel. He went after Loon, who kept blazing at him. Once the small gun clicked empty, Loon pulled out the extra magazine that he had for it. He smacked the magazine into the bottom of his weapon, and as soon as he pointed it, the Mercury swung its front end around.

"Ooooh, shit!" Loon's eyes lit up and his eyebrows rose.

Thunk!

He went flying over the hood of the Mountaineer and landed on his back on the front lawn of his home, wincing. Lying there bawling, he heard Cuba coming back around in his truck. He also heard the police sirens closing in on their location. Peeling his eyelids back open, he looked to the street and saw the Mountaineer speeding in his direction. The grill of the SUV and its blinding headlights were moving in fast. Seeing this ignited a fire under his ass. Scrambling to his feet as fast as he could, Loon limped towards his house with the truck closing the distance between them hastily. Feeling the behemoth on his heels, the nigga dove for the porch of his home. He landed on the porch and knocked the wind out of his stomach, just as the truck crashed into the steps.

"Fuck!" Cuba slammed his fist down on the steering wheel. When he heard the police sirens again and saw the colorful lights flashing from his right, he looked over his shoulder and found a couple of police cars heading in his direction. He knew right then that he had to get the fuck up from out of there before they were able to catch up with him. At the same time that Cuba was turning around and speeding off down the street, Loon was limping inside of his house and slamming the door shut behind him.

Chapter Nine

Loon was lucky to have escaped the firefight with Cuba. He'd left the battle with a shoulder wound and aching back having been hit by a truck. Homie had managed to flee the house just as the police arrived on the scene. He made his way out of the backdoor into his backyard and hopped the fence into the alley. Coming out from the opposite end of the alley, he secured a Chevy Monte Carlo for his transportation. He knew exactly where that nigga Cuba laid his head. He stayed on the other side of the city in a two bedroom house in Glendale. If he was lucky he'd find him there, if not, he was sure his baby momma would be there. He was going to snatch her ass up and call for Cuba's head. This would make his job a hell of a lot easier.

***

Cuba walked into the 76 gas station's rest room with a white plastic bag and shut the door behind him, locking it. He walked over to the sink and took the items he purchased out of the bag, sitting them on the sink. There was Tylenol, peroxide, gauze, tape and a pair of tweezers. Cuba took off his hoodie and sat it on the lid of the commode. Next, he removed the shirt he wore over his wife beater. When he done this, he found his gunshot wound on his shoulder. Wincing, he turned from left to right observing himself in his reflection. Pulling his blue bandana from his left back pocket, he folded it up and bit down on it hard. He then picked up the tweezers and took a deep breath, blowing hot air from his nose. He eased the tweezers inside of his wound and probed around for the bullet. He squeezed his eyelids shut and veins bulged at his temples. Cuba growled like an angry dog, trying to combat the pain. Tears outlined his eyelashes and slid down his cheeks. The young killa continued to probe his wound; finally, he discovered the bullet. Slowly, he pulled the slug out and held it up before his eyes. Taking the bandana from out of his mouth, he stood there observing it. It was stained crimson.

"So, you're the lil'fucka that's been givin' me hell, huh?" Cuba dropped the bullet into the sink and poured a few on the Tylenol into his palm. After he tossed them back, he turned on the faucet and used the water to wash the pills down. Having done this, he went about the task of dressing his wound. Once he was done, he taped the gauze over the area that had been injured.

He placed his hands on either side of the sink and leaned forward, staring at himself in the mirror. "Man, a nigga could use a blunt right now, fa real."

At that precise moment, Cuba's cellular rung and vibrated inside of his pocket. He pulled it out. Seeing home on his screen, he just knew that it was his baby momma, so he went ahead and answered it.

"'Hey, baby." he spoke jovially into the cell phone

***

Stephanie sat on the commode with her panties around her ankles, talking on the cordless telephone. She cradled the phone to her ear with her shoulder, while holding either side of her protruding belly. A smile spread across her face, thinking about the life growing inside of her. She was six months pregnant with a baby girl. She and her fiancé, Cuba, planned on naming her Edith. This was his grandmother's name. He'd chosen to christen his baby girl with this name in her honor.

"Girl, you know Cuba's ass, he's ripping and running the streets as always." Stephanie told her friend when she asked about her baby's daddy. "Yeah, that's what he claims, but until I gotta ring on my finger, I'm not believing a damn thang, you feel me? Hold on." She sat the cordless down on the porcelain sink and wiped herself, flushing the toilet. Having done this, she turned on the faucet and the water flowed into the bowl easily. Afterwards, she lathered her hands with soap until they were white all over and rinsed them off under the flowing water. Once she was done, she dried her hands off on one of the towels on the rack and opened the door, heading out into the hallway. "Hell naw, this is it for me for a while, I already told Cuba that I'm not pushing out no more babies until I'm wearing his last name. Shiiiiit, a bitch ain't tryna stay a baby momma forever, you hear what I'm saying?"

Coming down the hallway, Stephanie made a left into the kitchen. Still talking to her bestie, she stood on the tips of her toes and opened up the cupboard. She took down a glass pitcher to make some Kool-Aid and walked over to counter. After ripping open two blue berry packets and pouring its contents inside of the pitcher along with a couple of scoops of sugar, she made her way over to the refrigerator. There, she opened the freezer, and a cold fog rolled out into her face. She paid it no mind as she gathered a few ice cubes and dropped them down inside of the pitcher.

"Girl, I can't fit any of my old clothes, my feet down swelled up something awful and my big ass is waddling around her like a goddamn duck."

"Well, bitch youz a duck then, lemme hear you quack!" her bestie said playfully.

"Woof! Woof! Woof!"

"Hoe, that's a dog, how the fuck you don't know how a mothafuckin' duck sound?"

Stephanie had just dropped the last of the ice cubes into the pitcher, when her and her homegirl busted up laughing at her response. Stephanie laughed so hard that tears ran from the corners of her eyes and she wiped them away with her thumbs.

"Gina, yo' crazy ass got me over here crying laughing, youz a mothafucking fool, for real." She shut the freezer and turned around, her eyes stretched wide open in terror and her stomach dropped. The telephone slipped out of her hand and fell to the surface. Little momma was standing face to face with a scowling Loon. She looked down and saw the .32 at his side, and swallowed the lump of fear that formed in her throat.

"Stephanie? Stephanie? Are you there?" Gina called out to her best friend.

"What's up?"

Stephanie's face twisted into a mask of anger. With a grunt, she swung the glass pitcher with all of her might at Loon's head and it exploded, sending glass flying everywhere. Her victim crashed to the floor and she ran towards the front door, her bare feet smacking against the kitchen floor. Moaning in pain, Loon got to his feet holding the side of his head. When he looked to his fingers they were slicked with blood. Dizzy, he looked up to see Stephanie running towards the front door. He made his way over to her, seeing her struggle to unchain and unlock the door. She'd just pulled the door open when he kicked it back shut and grabbed a fist full of her individual braids. Yanking her head back and making her howl in pain, he slammed her face first into the door. The impact made her fall back on the carpet, her eyelids flickered white and she moaned.

"Stephaniee! Stephanieee! Stephanieee!" Gina continued to call out to her best friend.

Loon limped over into the kitchen and picked up the cordless telephone. Breathing heavily, he placed the phone to his ear and said, "She'll call you back." He disconnected the call and opened up the cabinet underneath the kitchen sink. He rummaged through the cleaning products that were there until he found what he was looking for: duct-tape. Having gotten the item that he was looking for, he picked up the dish rag and headed into the living room. He used the duct-tape to restrain Stephanie's wrists and gagged her mouth with a dish rag. Once he was done, he picked up the cordless and called that nigga Cuba up.

"Hey, baby." Cuba came on the line.

"What's cracking, bitch-boy?" Loon smiled satanically.

"Fuck is this?"

"Fuck you think, lil' nigga? Now, listen up, I got cho baby momma right her on the floor, knocked out cold. I plan on putting one in her head, but I won't if you do what I tell you to do. Here's what I want chu to do, take yo' strap and blow yo' mothafucking brains out."

"Fuck you, nigga! You ain't got my baby momma; put her on the phone then."

Loon looked to Stephanie and she was just coming to. He pulled the gag down from out of her mouth and held the phone to her ear, while placing his .32 to her temple. Once she gathered her wits, he told her exactly what to do.

"Yo' punk ass baby's daddy is on the phone, tell that mark ass nigga that I got a banger to yo' dome and if he don't do like I told 'em, I'ma shoot chu in the head and then I'ma shoot that lil' bitch growing in yo' stomach. Now, tell 'em what I said."

"Baby, I'm…I'm at the house and this nigga Loon has a gun to my head. He says if you don't do like…like he told you he's gonna kill me and the baby." Stephanie trembled, her eyes teary and heart thudding.

With that said, Loon put the gag back in her mouth and pressed the cordless to his ear. "You got that, champ? Now, do like the fuck I told you 'fore I make good on my threat."

"Bitch ass nigga, you always tryna pop somethin'. What? You scared to get it from the shoulders? Let's meet up and throw them hands, sucka! Let's chunk 'em to the death. If I lose then I'm dead like you want me, but if I'm the victor, then I walk away with Stephanie. How about it, nigga? You tryna see me in the streets? Or are you too chicken shit to squabble?"

Loon thought on it, scratching his temple with his .32, his eyes focused out of their corners. He had an ego as big as the goddamn Good Year blimp and his gangster coming under question didn't sit well with him. His reputation meant everything under the sun to him, and he wasn't about to let some young ass nigga challenge him and he back down. Fuck that. He'd never turned down a fade in his life and he wasn't about to start that night.

"All right then, bitch-boy, from the shoulders it is. Meet me at this address," he gave him the address and disconnected the call, tossing the cordless telephone aside on the couch.

***

Cuba pulled up to the location that Loon had told him to meet him. Jumping out of a '93 Acura that he'd procured for that night, he slammed his door shut and looked around. He found himself in between two tall ass warehouses that seemed to tower over him. He felt like an ant standing between the

154

buildings. The warehouses were empty and their windows were so dirty that you couldn't see in or out of them. From the looks of them, Cuba could tell that no one had been working in them for quite some time. He figured that they'd both had been shut down for whatever reason. Instantly, he knew why Loon had picked the location. There wasn't anyone down there besides the occasional homeless person. If they weren't sleeping on the sidewalks then they were pushing around shopping carts, gathering cans and bottles, and anything else they could recycle for cash.

Cuba pulled out his gun and checked its magazine. Seeing that it was fully loaded, he smacked it back into the bottom of the weapon and chambered a live hollow-tip round into it. Next, he stashed it back on his waistline and glanced at his watch. Loon was supposed to have been there twenty minutes ago but he'd yet to show his face. Cuba couldn't help wondering what the fuck could have happened. His first thought was that he'd walked straight into an ambush, but then he thought better of it. See, all of the hitters that Loon rolled with were officially dead. Hell, he'd saw to that himself, so a setup was out of the question. Cuba pulled out his cellular. He was about to bang that nigga'z line, until he was blinded by a pair of shining orbs. The headlights shining in his face caused him to squint and hold his hand above his brows. Once the headlights died and he saw Loon behind the wheel of a Chevy Monte Carlo that had stopped ten feet away from him, he slid he cell phone back inside of his pocket. The driver's door swung opened and Loon emerged, slamming the door shut behind him. He limped over to the grill of his stolen vehicle, a wicked smile plastered on his face.

Seeing that he had his .32 down at his side, Cuba brandished his piece again.

"Where's my baby's momma?" the young killa scowled.

"Follow me," Loon motioned for him to follow him, turning to walk around the car.

"I'm not going with you anywhere until you tuck that burner."

"After you," Cuba tucked his banger and Loon did the same. He then followed him to the trunk of the Monte Carlo. He watched as the lunatic, still keeping his eyes on him, knocked on the trunk. As soon as he did, he cupped his hand around his ear and waited to hear a sound. He got it when whoever was inside bumped around and he heard their muffled cries. "And there you have it."

"Nah, fuck that, lemme see her, it could be anybody in there." Cuba said, not trying fall for the bullshit.

"Smart nigga," Loon tapped his finger to his temple and then popped the trunk. When he lifted it open, he motioned

Cuba over so that he could take a look at the prize that he had inside. Cuba cautiously peeked over inside of the trunk, seeing his gagged and wrist bounded baby momma. She had terrified eyes and wet cheeks from crying. She tried to shout something to him, but the gag in her mouth muffled her words. Cuba promised her that he was going to get her out of the situation alive and Loon slammed the trunk on him, stashing the keys inside of his pocket. "All right, let's do this shit."

"Toss yo' strap, nigga."

"Unh unh, same time," Loon pulled out his piece at the same time that his opponent did. They held the weapons out by their side and then they dropped them, one after the other. The metal guns clasped to the ground. Afterwards, the two combatants peeled off their coats and shirts, tossing them aside. They then tightened their belts and laced their sneakers tighter than they were before. They did all of this keeping their eyes on one another, making sure the other didn't try anything. Once they were done they stood tall, bending their neck from side to side and cracking their knuckles. Lifting their fists, they moved around one another, looking for the flaw in one another's technique.

Seeing an opening, Loon launched his attack with fists of fury. He hit Cuba hard with a left, a right, and then an upper cut that lifted him off of his feet and dropped him on his ass.

He then stepped back, all the while keeping his eyes on his opponent. He watched as Cuba scrambled to get upon his feet and fell down repeatedly. The young killa had a look on his face that showed that he was dazed.

"Unh huh, these ain't the hands you want, lil' homie, I told you." Loon smirked arrogantly. "Come on now, get up, get on up, I'm not done witcho young ass yet." He moved around, observing Cuba as he shook off his daze and got to his feet. The youngster threw up his fists and moved in, throwing a couple of jabs. Loon dodged them with ease and faked a left, coming back with two well placed jabs of his own. The blows busted his opponent's lip and bloodied his nose. Cuba swung on him and he ducked, coming back up with haymakers that dropped him again. "I gotta say, baby boy, I am sorely disappointed with you. You ain't got no hands, you all trigga, my nigga. That's what's wrong with chu 90s babies, all you lil' niggaz know how to do is shoot!"

Cuba got up on his kneeling knee, pissed the fuck off. He wiped the blood that dripped from his nose with his fist. Seeing the smear of blood on his hand enraged him, he saw through a haze of red he was so angry. His eyebrows dipped and his lips peeled back in a sneer, making him look like an irate dog.

"Fuck you! Ahhhhhhh!" he charged at Loon screaming, grabbing him by his waist. Once that nigga started laying blows to the back of Cuba's skull, the young killa swung around to the back of him. Holding him tightly by the waist, with a grunt, he lifted Loon's ass up and slammed him on his head. Cuba then released him and jumped back, lifting up his fists. Standing back, he watched as his opponent, while in a daze, attempted to get on his feet.

"Get up, gone and get up, mothafucka! I'm not finished yet." Cuba talked that shit to him like he was talking earlier. Once Loon had finally got upon one of his knees, the young killa moved in and kicked him hard as shit across the jaw. The force behind the impact sent a mist of blood flying through the air. Loon fell on his back, small streams of blood running from either sides of his mouth. He stared wide eyed up into the sky, tongue moving around in a mouth full of blood, tasting metal. He spat out three red teeth and slowly got to his feet, nearly falling six times. Although Loon managed to lift his fists, he saw two Cuba's standing before him. Still, he advanced in his direction, throwing punches. The youngster moved swiftly, seeing his opponent's fists before they even came. Seeing an opening for him to launch his attack, Cuba took full advantage of it.

Bwap! Bop! Wop!

Cuba finished Loon off with an upper cut. The impact of the blow threw Loon's head back and sent him up in the air, slamming down flat on his back. He lay there with his eyelids shut, turning his head from left to right. His face was wincing and he was moaning. Cuba's shadow was cast over him as he stood erect, mad dogging him. Spitting off to the side, he picked up his blazer and tucked it on his waistline. He then popped the trunk and walked around to the rear of the Chevy. When he lifted the trunk, he found his weeping baby's momma staring up at him. Cuba pulled the gag from out of her mouth and used his teeth to tear the duct-tape that bound her wrists. Taking her by the hand, he helped her step out of the trunk and onto the pavement. She hugged and kissed him, tears continuously sliding down her cheeks.

"Shhhhhhh," Cuba hushed the woman that was to give birth to his first child. He rubbed her back and kissed the side of her face. "It's gonna be okay, baby. It's all over now." He said, holding her at arm's length, watching her wipe away the tear that threatened to fall from her eye. "How's my baby." He rubbed her protruding belly, a smile etched across his face.

"She's okay." Stephanie managed a halfhearted smile, looking down at her stomach and holding either side of it.

"Good, stay here, I'll be right back." Cuba kneeled down to her stomach, rubbing on it happily and then kissing it.

Afterwards, he walked towards an unconscious Loon, his menacing eyes focused on him. While en route to him, he unbuckled his leather belt and pulled it free from the loops of his jeans. Next, he opened the driver side door of his enemy's car and drugged him over to it. Having taken the keys to the Monte Carlo out of Loon's pocket, he put it into the ignition and turned it so that the symbols on the dashboard light up. He then put the vehicle in neutral. Right after, he looped the belt around Loon's wrist and pulled it tight, its buckle biting into his wrist. Afterwards, he tied the end of the belt to the steering wheel of the car and shifted it into drive. He pushed the rear of the car and then stood up, watching it slowly roll forward. With the vehicle still in motion, Loon slowly began to come around. His eyelids twitched and fluttered open. He looked to the arm that was tied to the steering wheel of his whip and then at his sneakers. He kicked his legs wildly as he was pulled down the street. Beyond his sneakers he saw Cuba standing in the middle of the street, watching him attentively. Seeing that he was in danger, Loon screamed for help as loud as he could. He screamed over and over again until his voice went hoarse. No longer able to scream, Loon reached above his head trying to release his wrist from the belt that held him bound to the steering wheel. He'd managed to get to his feet, but he ended up falling again because the car had picked up speed. Again, he tried to get up but his efforts were futile. The Monte Carlo was moving too fast for him, so he lost his equilibrium repeatedly.

Cuba whipped out his blazer and held it down at his side, watching his enemy as he was pulled down the street. Having taken a deep breath, he gripped his gun with both hands and lifted it. Shutting his right eyelid and angling his head to the side, he aimed his weapon and gave the trigger a squeeze. The bullet flew out of the barrel in what appeared to be slow motion, spinning while en route to its intended target. The bullet went through the back of the Chevy and entered its gas tank. Instantly, the vehicle exploded and fire swept over it, igniting Loon into flames. He screamed in agony and danced in the street as he was pulled along. His Monte Carlo crashed into a parked Astro van. Loon continued to dance on the side of his car, fire devouring his form and incinerating his flesh. He screamed louder and louder. Soon his movements grew slower until they eventually stopped and he lay still. He was dead. The fire from the wrecked car spread to the Astro van and heated up its gas tank. Suddenly, both vehicles exploded, sending burning wreckage and body parts flying everywhere. A burning leg was the first to come smacking down on the street. Next, was an arm, which came down on the hood of a Ford F-150. Loon's severed head was the last to fall, landing dead smack at Cuba's feet. It burned, looking like a hunk of charcoal, still holding the mold of Loon screaming.

"Baby?" Hearing a voice at his back, Cuba whipped around and pointed his gun. This startled his baby momma; she gasped and threw her hands over her chest. Slowly, Cuba lowered his weapon at his side. He was so engrossed in his fight with Loon that he'd forgotten that he'd removed her restraints and let her out of the trunk. "You, okay?"

"Yeah, I'm straight." He tucked his gun at the front of his jeans and she hugged him, wrapping her arms around him. She peered over his shoulder at the fire behind them, seeing Loon's burning body and the vehicles as well. She shut her eyelids and tears slid down her cheeks, as she rubbed her hand up and down her man's back lovingly.

Chapter Ten

Smurf and a group of his niggaz kicked hood politics hanging on the corner. Bottles of liquor and smoldering blunts were rotated around them, smoke lingering in their presence. Most of them were tipsy and high, while the rest of them were on point just in case any drama arose. The better part of the night they spent curb serving, but once they realized that the crackheads weren't really fucking with that work that they had on deck, they decided to just pull together and get saucy.

A Dodge Neon pulled to a jerking halt before the curb. Instantly, fools highs were blown and they sobered up. Smurf and his niggaz went for the bulges on their waistline. They were about to pull out and soak whoever was behind the wheel of the old car up, but that nigga Smurf identified who was in the driver seat. Taking note of who it was, he threw up his hand and dropped the hand that he was reaching for the gun on him with by his side.

"Y'all niggaz be easy, that's that nigga Gar, man." He announced to them, his O-Dog like braids hanging just over his eyebrows. This made his eyes look spooky and dangerous. Smurf was a little nigga that had gotten his name from his height and the fact that he was so black that he was blue. It was cold out so he was dressed in a bomber jacket with beige fur around the hood. He also sported a gold necklace that held to a bust of one of the Smurfs from the cartoon series. This piece of jewelry dangled out of the collar of his jacket, hanging at his chest.

The door of the Neon swung opened and Gar emerged, planting the foot of his damaged leg on the pavement. He looked over the roof of his vehicle, taking in the appearance of all of the fools present that were a part of Lafayette's operation.

"'Sup, ya'll?" he threw his head back.

"What up, my nigga? Niggaz thought you were dead, for real." Smurf told him. The niggaz that were with him exchanged glances and nodded. They all heard about him getting blasted on that night by Auntie and Diana. Although he was laid up in a coma, niggaz laid it on thick making the hood believe that he'd kicked the bucket.

"Nah, I'm alive. A lil' banged up, but a nigga will make it." He assured them, "Y'all out here getting money?"

"Shit slow as molasses, dawg." Blowl spoke up. He was a little nigga that was a tad bit taller than Smurf. He had six neat cornrows which were braided to the back and tied off by rubber bands. He was rocking a hoodie and skinny jeans.

"Slow as a mothafucka," Champ added his two scents. He was a long neck light skinned cat that rocked a beanie and black jean suit. "Ever since you and that nigga La been gone, we been out here rocking with this ol' bullshit tryna make something of it."

"Real spit, this new shit we got, runnin' the mothafuckin' crackheads off and shit," This one nigga named Duck said. He had a brown hue and rocked a bunch of funny ass designs in his fade.

"Okay, check this out," Gar began. He went on to give the young niggaz the rundown on Lafayette being killed in County and the plug being snatched. He told them that he was planning on getting her back but he was going to need their help. "I could really use some extra guns on this shit. So what's up? Y'all gone back me? Or is a G gone have to move out on some solo shit?"

"Give us a minute," Smurf threw up a finger, signaling for Gar to give him a minute. He huddled up with the rest of his homeboys and they chopped it up. Gar could hear their soft whispers and hushed tones as they engaged in their conversation. He folded his arms across his chest and waited for their discussion to come to an end. Finally, the huddle dismantled and Smurf stepped forth, clearing his throat with his fist to his mouth. He swallowed the excess spit in his mouth before beginning. "If we roll out on this shit and get the plug back, is she gone bless the streets so niggaz can eat again?"

"Homegirl is very generous. I know for a fact, if y'all help me save her ass, she gone make sure anybody down with La's old crew is straight. I guarantee that." He crossed himself in the sign of the crucifix and kissed his fingers, throwing them up to God Almighty.

Smurf looked to his homeboys to his left and right, they nodded. "All right then, we riding." The young nigga dapped up Gar. He chopped it up with them a while longer and then they all hopped into a couple of Hummers, piling up in them and pulling off. Their first step was to go pick up the guns that they had stashed. Afterwards, they were going to track down Victoria and bring her home.

***

Thoom!

Koom!

Two Hummers came crashing through the enormous gates of Diablo's estate, one by one. Sitting on top of the huge vehicles and armed with AK-47s, were Duck and Blowl. The rest of the homies were inside. They were armed up with them high powered thangs too, ready to bring it to the drug lord and his men and rescue the lady that could make it snow in the streets for them again. The Hummers came racing over the gates, one after another. That nigga Gar was the last man in, flooring a Pontiac Grand Am over the threshold. The car went two feet into the air and came slamming down it was going so fast. Debris and pieces of the lawn went up into the air, but he kept on going. Homeboy had determination in his eyes and hatred in his heart. Keeping his eyes on what was ahead of him; he reached over into the front passenger seat and grabbed the AK-47 he'd brought along for the mission.

The Mexican men with the AK-47s on top of the mansion made to point their weapons down at the approaching hummers. The double doors of the mansion came flying open and more Mexicans came pouring out, choppas blazing. The hummers came to a halt on the lawn, the windshields of the enormous vehicles cracked into cobwebs as they took the copper jacketed bullets. The niggaz inside of the Hummers jumped out. Some of them took cover behind the vehicles and opened fire from where they were, taking some of the Mexicans off of their feet. Some of the niggaz behind the Hummers got taken out too, receiving fire from the fools on the mansion.

Blatatatatatatatatatatat!

Smurf ran across the lawn, taking some of the Mexican fools out that were on the rooftop of the mansion. One of them fell towards the ground screaming at the top of his lungs before slamming into the surface. When he hit the ground, the young nigga and the boy Blowl tatted him up with them thangs, making sure his bitch ass was dead.

"I'm going around back to the master bedroom, cover my ass." Smurf called out to Blowl. He then took off running, lighting up some of the Mexicans as he went along.

"You won't some, come get some, pussies!" Blowl gritted from behind a ski-mask. His arms shook as he cut loose with that big ass AK-47. The cries and hollers of his enemies filled his eardrums. This didn't stop the youngsta though; he kept on dumping at him. Hot bullets ripped through warm bodies, mangling legs and taking off arms. Blood and bone fragments flew as the enemy met with death.

Blatatatatatatatatatatat!

Gar hopped out of the Grand Am, leaving the driver's door open. He ducked for cover, hearing bullets tat up his stolen vehicle. Broken glass went flying and the side view mirror exploded. He got down on his knees and looked beneath the driver's door. Seeing the booted feet of Diablo's men, he swept his choppa across them. A spray of bullets had their asses screaming bloody murder, having had their ankles cut in half. When they fell to the lawn, Gar's comrades surged forward and painted them in blood with their assault rifles. While they were doing this, they got some hot shit sent their way.

"Ahhhhhh!"

"Gaahh!"

"Raaahh!"

They met with their bloody demise and hit the ground full of holes. Those that were left went charging up the steps inside of the mansion, firing away on the Mexicans inside. Within the walls of the mansion, thunder erupted back to back. The men went at it with the automatic weaponry, bodies dropping on both sides. Suddenly, the gunfire ceased and smoke clouded the inside, billowing out onto the front porch.

Blowl removed the banana clip from out of his choppa and reloaded that bitch. He then looked to Gar and said, "Big homie, you good?"

Gar looked around at all of the dead bodies lying sprawled on the lawn. There were both comrades and enemies lying dead.

"Yeah, I'm straight." Gar nodded.

"How we gone…" Blowl was cut short by a wave of gunfire going straight across his chest. His eyelids squeezed shut and he hollered out in excruciation. He staggered forward, involuntarily firing his AK-47 at the ground and creating a dirt cloud. As he collapsed to the ground, Gar looked in the direction that the fire came from. At the end of his line of vision, he found one of the Mexicans there that had gotten shot down from the rooftop of the mansion. He lay where he was bleeding at the chest and the mouth, outstretched hand pointing an assault rifle at him.

"Mothaaafuuuckaaa!" Gar bellowed, pointing his AK-47 at the nigga that had chopped down Blowl. He pulled the trigger of the deadly weapon and it rattled to life in his hands. His arms jerked back and forth. The assault rifle spat hot fire and blasted the Mexican's chest and skull apart. His face and head looked like a busted water melon once the jacketed bullets were through with him.

***

Diablo sat behind the desk in his bedroom with his boots kicked upon the desk top, smoking the world's biggest cigar. His eyes were focused on the device in his hands. It was the size of a PSP video game system, and had several small screens on it. These individual screens were hooked up to the surveillance cameras that surrounded his mansion. They showed him everything going on inside and outside of it. Anyone went to go do anything; he'd see their monkey asses. Whenever he wanted to see a certain area inside or outside of his estate, all he had to do was tap one of the small screens to enlarge it.

Diablo had just taken a big drag from his overgrown cancer stick and blew out smoke into the air, when he saw the hummers and the Grand Am running down the gates of his home. His eyes bulged and he damn near choked on the bit of smoke that he had left in his throat. Hastily, he sat up where he was perched and grabbed his walkie talkie, alerting the few men that he had on the grounds that they were under attack. Afterwards, he smacked the walkie talkie down on the desk top and sprung to his feet, grabbing a .44 Magnum revolver. Quickly, he holstered the firearm and picked up the M-16 that was lying up against his desk. Switching hands with the cigar, he racked a jacketed bullet into the assault rifle. With that out of the way, he ran to the double doors of his study and yanked them open. He then ran out onto the terrace, releasing hell on the men that invaded his kingdom.

"You cock suckers, come into my domain, eh? Eat this!" he hollered down below to the niggaz that scattered throughout his mansion as soon as they crossed the threshold.

Blatatatatatatatatatatatatatatat!

"Ahhhhh!"

"Gaaah!"

"Argh!"

They screamed out in agony as hot shit passed in and out of their bodies, turning their clothing crimson.

***

Smurf crawled over the railing and onto the terrace. He smiled wickedly behind the black bandana that covered the lower half of his face, when he saw Diablo with his back to him, firing on the homies downstairs. Moving with stealth, he made his way over to the glass door and slid it open quietly. Crossing the threshold, he slung his AK-47 over his shoulder and unsheathed the machete that was dangling on his hip. Now, he could have taken the drug lord out with the assault rifle, but he wanted his head, and the only way he was going to get it was with that machete, which he brought along for the ride.

Tip toeing over to Diablo while his back was turned to him, Smurf pulled the bandana down from the lower half of his face. He licked his lips in anticipation of his kill. Once he had the infamous man's severed head, the entire hood would be talking about him for years to come. He'd be a fucking legend in the streets.

Smurf was about three feet away from Diablo when he lifted the machete. A gleam swept up the length of the sharp blade and it sparkled at its tip. He took one more step forward and the carpet squeaked. Diablo's head snapped around to the young nigga and he scowled. Swiftly, he swung around and kicked him in the stomach. The impact knocked the wind out of him, and he dropped the blade. When Smurf doubled over and hugged his self, he looked up and the butt of the assault rifle came slamming into his forehead. The blow knocked him on his back, leaving him grimacing. While he wallowed in pain, Diablo tossed his empty AK-47 aside and drew his .44 Magnum revolver, cocking back its hammer with his thumb. After spitting what was left of his cigar off to the sidelines, he shot Smurf in his shoulder, causing him to holler out in agony. Afterwards, he holstered his wafting pistol and snatched the sheets off of his bed, tying them to make a homemade noose. Hearing someone at the door, he whipped around and put one right through their chest. It was Duck. He staggered backwards and flipped over the railing, snapping his neck upon impact of the shiny floor below. His choppa lay a few feet away from him.

Having re-holstered his revolver, Diablo used a pillowcase to bound Smurf's wrists behind his back and tied the noose around his neck. Next, he dragged him out to the terrace and tied the sheet around the railing. Taking a step back, he drew his .44 again and pointed it at his back.

***

Gar moved through the gun smoke of the mansion, stepping over dead bodies and shit. His choppa was braced against his shoulder and his head was on a swivel, moving along with it. He was in search of Diablo. He knew that he had to get to him if he wanted to find Victoria and get the fuck from out of there.

A sharp, loud whistle from above stole his attention and he looked up. He was about to open fire until he saw Smurf. The young nigga was standing before the guard railing, bleeding at the shoulder. He had a noose made out of bed sheets tied around his neck and his wrists were bound behind his back by a pillowcase. His eyelids were narrowed into slits and he was gritting to combat the fire where he had been shot. Directly behind him, stood a scowling Diablo with his .44 Magnum revolver pointed at his back. His eyebrows were arched and his jaws were locked, showcasing the muscles in his face.

"You fucked up!" Diablo roared at Gar.

"Let 'em go!" he yelled back up at him.

"Gaaarrrrrr!" Smurf hollered out for his big homie's help.

"You fucked up big time!" Diablo roared again.

"Let 'em go, mothafucka!" Gar yelled back up to him again.

"As you wish!" he smiled satanically and kicked Smurf in the back. The impact from the blow sent his ass flipping over the railing and hurling towards the floor, screaming to the top of his lungs. The bed sheet unraveled quickly and then straightened, snagging him at the opposite end. The swung back and forth fast, slowly slowing his momentum.

"Smuurrrf, nooooo," Gar lowered his choppa and climbed the staircase as fast as he could. On his way up the staircase, he saw that nigga Diablo run back inside of his bedroom and slam the door shut. He didn't pay him any mind because his attention was focused on helping Smurf. He went to lay his choppa up against the railing until someone took a shot at him. A spray of bullets went past his ear, missing it by half an inch.

Meanwhile, Smurf's eyes lit up and veins bulged at his temples and neck, feeling the sheet tightened around his windpipe. He thrashed around on the homemade noose, trying his damndest to loosen the restraint around his throat. He kicked his legs wildly and pissed his jeans, a yellow stream splashing on the surface. The urine pitter patted the floor until it fell in trickles and then dripped. His movements grew slower and slower.

Blatatatatatatatat!

Gar returned fire at the Mexican fool down stairs that had just tried to take his head off. He ducked down behind the railing and peered down at Smurf, who was still dangling about, movements growing slower and slower.

"Hold on, Smurf, just hold on!" he yelled down to his little homie.

Blatatatatat!

The rapid fire took his attention off of Smurf. He couldn't rescue him if he was dead, so saving his own ass was of the upmost importance right then.

Once the fire had ceased, Gar looked down and saw that the Mexican man was ejecting the spent banana clip from his AK-47 and moving to reload another one. Now was his time to react. Jumping up from where he was stooped, he sprayed some hot shit at him. The mothafucka ran, tucked and rolled, nearly being struck by the heat wave that was meant to take his life. He was out of Gar's sight, but he did hear a door shut somewhere far off inside of the mansion. Pulling his choppa back up, Gar looked over the railing and found Smurf hanging from the homemade nose, slowly twisting from left to right as urine dripped from him on to the floor below.

"Damn, my nigga Smurf," Gar said, eyes full of sorrow. He smacked his lips hating to see that the young nigga was dead. He crossed himself in the sign of the crucifix and whipped around to Diablo's study's door. His face twisted in hatred and he locked his jaws, showcasing the bone structure in his face. Taking a deep breath, he turned to his right and kicked the door with all of his might. The door rattled, but it didn't come loose from its hinges. He kicked that mothafucka repeatedly but it still didn't budge. So, he said fuck it and fired on the lock of that bastard. The AK-47 clicked empty and the lock fell from out of the door, hitting the floor.

Gar tossed the AK-47 aside and brandished his .38 from the small of his back. Right after, he kicked the door open and sent it flying inward. His eyes scanned the study and he didn't see Diablo anywhere in sight. He knew that his brown ass was there though, because he could smell his bitch ass. The wind from the outside blew in and ruffled the curtains. In doing so, Diablo's hiding place was revealed.

"Peek-a-boo, I see you..."Gar smiled evilly.

Diablo's eyes stretched wide open and he ran out from his hiding place, exchanging fire with Gar.

Boom! Boom! Boom! Boom!

Pop! Pop!

Diablo gritted as he took one in the stomach. He stumbled backwards and fell up against the wall, sliding down to the floor and leaving a blood smear. He moaned in pain and kicked his right leg. Touching his wound, he looked at it and saw blood. When he looked up, Gar was moving in as fast as he could to finish him off. Seeing this, Diablo hoisted up his .44 Magnum revolver and tilted his head back, pressing it underneath his chin. He was about to pull the trigger, when Gar kicked his pistol from out of his hand. The revolver went flying across the room; Gar pointed his .38 at the drug lord's chest.

Pop! Pop!

Diablo's jerked twice from the shots and he slid off to the side. Lowering his blazer at his side, Gar took the time to study his handiwork before walking off. Coming out of the door, he went down the staircase, looking at Smurf as he hung. He shook his head sadly, and continued on his journey. Approaching the basement door, he heard the Mexican fool that had taken shots at him earlier promising death to anyone that dared to come down there. Still hearing homeboy talking shit, Gar calmly removed the small copper key on the small hook by the door and unlocked it. He pulled open the door and made his way down the staircase. He stopped halfway to the basement floor. Looking ahead, he saw the man's shadow casted on the wall. He was standing directly behind who he believed was Victoria with his choppa aimed at her back.

"I don't know who the fuck you mayates are," the Mexican man began in a thick South American accent. "But if you step one foot down here, I'm blowin' this puta's head off, yeah?"

"Boss lady?" Gar called out to the queen pin.

"Yeeaahhh?" she called out.

"Shut the fawk up!" he jabbed her in the back of the head with the barrel of the AK-47. She winced and hung her head.

"I'ma needa window of time." He responded, holding his revolver at his side, his back pressed against the wall.

"You...you got it." She winced, feeling throbbing at the back of her head.

"Fawk did I say, ju black bish?" the Mexican man hollered out and jabbed her in the back with his assault rifle.

"Now!" She flipped around and kicked the AK-47 that was held at her back. The Mexican man's arm swung upwards as he held back the trigger, spitting flames and causing debris to fall. As soon as he was given the signal, Gar jumped down three more steps and lifted his .38. Squeezing one eye shut, he let off a few shots.

Pop! Pop!

The Mexican man's shoulders danced taking the heat to his chest. The kill-shot was the hot one to his noodle, which sent his brain fragments flying out of the back of his dome. He crashed to the floor, his blood oozing out and outlining his form. His eyes were wide open, staring up at the ceiling.

"Is he through?"Gar called out.

Victoria looked behind her and saw that he was wearing The Face of Death. Quickly, she kicked the AK-47 from out of his reach, sending it sliding across the floor.

"Yeah, he's done." She called back out.

"All right, I'm coming down." Taking his time, Gar made it down the steps on his good leg. He approached Victoria, taking a look at the Mexican fool that he'd laid down and then looking back up at her. His brows furrowed seeing the number that Diablo and his men had done on her. They violated every hole on her body, but she was standing like the soldier that she was. He had to salute her. She was a straight up G.

"You, okay?"Gar inquired.

"If I told you that I was would you believe me?" she managed to crack a weak smile. Truthfully, she was hungry and exhausted. There wasn't a place on her that wasn't aching either.

"Nah, I couldn't say I would, let me get chu outta these shackles." He grabbed her shackled wrist. She looked up and her eyelids stretched opened wide, seeing someone standing behind him.

He whipped around and found Diablo. He was holding his bleeding chest and wincing. Lazily, he went to lift up his revolver and point it.

"Kiss your black ass goodbye!" he went to pull the trigger.

Bloc!

Half of his mothafucking head exploded and he hit the surface hard as fuck. His executioner stood over him, heating up his back with that act-right.

Bloc! Bloc! Bloc! Bloc!

The gunman lowered his banger and took a good look at the dead body he'd created, angling his head. He then looked up at Gar and Victoria, making his way in their direction.

"Slow yo' roll, Blood?" Gar scowled and pointed his .38, finger settled on the trigger. The nigga that he barked the order to didn't stop, he kept in their direction. The closer he moved towards them, the more of him that became visible until his identity was revealed.

"La...Lafayette?" Victoria gasped and peered closer. She couldn't believe that it was him.

"La? I thought...I thought you were dead." A shocked Gar said.

"The dead walk." He smiled from beneath the hood of his Nike track suit. His feet were comfortable in a pair of all white Air Force Ones. He paid a confidential source to recover his cell phone, which was linked to the GPS app that Victoria had on her cellular. Once he escaped from jail, he went to her mansion and saw that it was ruin. That's when he decided to use the app to track her down. He knew he didn't have the muscle to break her out of her homemade prison, and he didn't want to gather the gunners he knew to form an attack because he didn't want to reveal his being alive. With that in mind, he played the background trying to brainstorm a plan. That's when he gathered intelligence that Gar was leading an attack to rescue Victoria from her captors. He let them bust the doors down and then he swooped in, hoping he wasn't too late to save her ass.

"My mom's gotta call from the jail saying that you were killed." Gar informed him.

"Nah," he shook his head. "Niggaz took my twin brotha out. That was him. Luckily, I escaped when I did, or I'd be in his position."

Flashback

Lafayette's eyes fluttered open. His vision was blurry, but it came back into focus after a while. He gave himself the once over, seeing that he was bound to a chair by heavy silver chains. Although he was restrained, it didn't stop him from trying to get loose. His struggling caused the chair that he was perched in to slide slightly across the floor. He attempted this for a while and all it did was tire him, leaving him breathing hard. His chest inflated and deflated, as he inhaled and exhaled, looking about. He was inside of the shower room, which was dimly lit. He looked around for someone or something that would lead him to his salvation, but there wasn't

184

anyone or anything in sight. A moment later, he heard foot-steps come from his left. When he looked a correctional officer came to a stop inside of the doorway, standing off to the side. He looked in at the mothafucka bound to the chair and then folded his arms across his chest, leaning up against the doorway. Soon after there was whistling, drawing closer and closer. Then there was the sound of something metal being drug on the cement floor. The noise stopped at the door way. There was the silhouette of a short man carrying something long and curved at its end. He patted the C.O on the arm and stepped inside of the shower room, walking in Lafayette's direction. The closer he got to the hustler, the more he began to fill out under the dim lighting that the shower room provid-ed. The short man suddenly stopped before Lafayette. His face was partially hidden by the darkness of the room so the hustler peered closer to identify him. When recognition ripped through his brain, he had to blink a few times to be sure of who was standing before him.

"Lil…Lil…Lil…" he stammered.

"Lil Man, alive and in the mothafucking flesh," The little nigga smiled wickedly and tapped the pipe in his palm.

Lafayette was speechless, he couldn't believe it. A walking, talking, dead man stood right before his eyes.

"They had me caged up in P.C, after that amateur ass hit them pussies laid down." Lil Man put it out there. "Them folks put the word out that I was dead for my protection, them other niggaz never seen it coming when I put in the order to have 'em hit." Homie bound to the chair eyes doubled in size and his mouth formed an O, seeing the little nigga tapping the pipe into his palm. "You betrayed me; I would have rotted inside this shithole for you! It crushed me when I found out that it was you that put the green light on me! Disloyalty is a violation punishable by death! And your sentencing has come, Lafayette!" He brought the pipe above his head and brought it down with all of his might.

Cling! Crack!

Lafayette's chin slammed into his chest and the top of his skull cracked open like a mothafucking egg. His brain and blood bubbled out the top of his scalp, oozing down over his face. Lafayette's fingers and legs twitched, his tongue hung out of his mouth. Again, Lil Man brought the pipe down with all of his might, speckling his jumpsuit with blood. Again, again, and again, he struck down upon his enemy with hatred and furious anger. The powerful blows cracked Lafayette's skull open further and further, sending brain fragments sliding down his face and dropping wet into his lap. Lil Man brought his pipe down and allowed it to dangle at his side. He stared down at the mess he had created, chest rising and falling rapidly, mouth open as he took husky breaths. He spat off to the side and tossed the pipe aside.

"Rest in shit," Lil' Man's eyes lingered on his victim for a time. He was about to turn to walk away, when something caught his eyes. "What the fuck?" he uttered in disbelief. He couldn't believe his eyes; he thought his mind was playing tricks on him. He grabbed Lafayette by the lower half of his face and gave him a closer look. His eyes stretched wide open and he gasped. "8-Ball?" he identified Lafayette's twin brother by the dog paw tattooed at the corner of his eye. "This isn't him!" A frowning Lil' Man announced to the correctional officer.

"Bullshit, I know who the fuck I snatched up." The correctional officer stated. He was offended that the little nigga had come at him like he was a Master Fuck-up. He strolled over from where he was leant up against the doorway. He made his way across the room, the leather of his boots making noise against the floor. He was a stocky white cat with reddish blonde hair and hairy arms. The closer he got to Lil' Man the more of him that filled out under the dim light. He stopped before Lil' Man and the dead mothafucka who he believed was Lafayette.

The correctional officer pulled a mug shot from out of his back pocket. He held the dead nigga by the lower half of his face. Looking back and forth between the corpse's face and the mug shot of Lafayette, forehead creased with lines. Although the person restrained in the chair and the one in the mug shot were spot on, they differed in a slightly different hair style and tattoo.

"Shiiiiiit," he shoved the photo into his back pocket and addressed Lil' Man. "This isn't him."

"No shit. But where in the hell is he?" Lil' Man asked concerned.

Meanwhile

Lafayette found his eyelids growing heavier and heavier with each minute that passed by until they eventually shut. The nigga was asleep when the door of his cell was unlocked and a correctional officer stepped inside. He made his way over to him and stopped at the head of his bed. In his hands he had a pair of polished black leather boots and a correctional officer's uniform.

"Aye, it's time to rock and roll." With that said, Lafayette's eyelids peeled back open, and when he saw the C.O, he shot to his feet. In a hurry, he peeled off his jump suit and got dressed in the uniform presented to him. Once he was clad in the clothing, he took the utility belt that he was given and put

it on. Afterwards, the correctional officer that gave him the uniformed balled up the jumpsuit and shoved it inside of a shopping mall bag. He nudged Lafayette and the two of them made their way out of the cell and shut it closed.

That night, Lafayette walked out of the County jail with no problems, dressed as a civilian and wearing a disguise of course. Still, he was a free man and able to do as he pleased. It cost him a pretty big bag to spring him free from The Beast, but it was well worth it seeing as how he was looking at life imprisonment.

Present

See, Lafayette had always been a business man. He was blessed with a brain and the gift of gab, so he knew how to negotiate. As soon as he got behind the wall and saw this correctional officer he used to sell nickel bags of Sess to back in high school, he presented him with a scheme that would guarantee that he walked and all parties involved would get paid handsomely. Although the move left him damn near broke, Lafayette rationalized that a real hustler could lose it all and get it back. And he was a *real* hustler.

Lafayette took in Victoria's appearance, lines formed on his forehead. "What happened to you, Vic?"He caressed the side of her face, looking over the injuries that covered her body. He also smelled the feces and urine that filled the air, but he didn't mention it for fear of embarrassing her. It didn't take a rocket scientist to see that she had been raped and sodomized.

"What didn't happen to me?" the queen pin spoke seriously. She shut her eyelids and tilted her head, rubbing her cheek against the palm of his hand.

"I'm sorry about all of this. If it hadn't been for me asking you to help me smash these fools, then you wouldn't have been…"

"Shhhhhh, never mind all of that. You just help me get outta here." She told him.

"You got it." Lafayette replied, kissing her lips lovingly. He then tucked his gun inside of his sweatpants. He took her by her shackled wrist and looked over the restraint. A gleam swept around the length of it. "We gone have to shoot chu free of these chains."

"Hold up, homie may have the key on 'em." Gar said of a dead Diablo.

"If not, we're blasting these bitches off." Lafayette spoke of the chains that held Victoria.

"While you saving them, who the fuck gone save you?" A familiar voice rang out from behind the trio. Lafayette's eyes were the first to stretch wide open, then there was Victoria's and Gar's. All of their heads turned at once, seeing a dark figure moving in their direction, pulling out something the shape of a gun. Seeing this, Lafayette went to point his .9mm, but he was far too late on the draw. Whomever homie was approaching had the drop on that ass. His tool was already up spitting hot fire.

Blocka!

The first shot sent Lafayette's .9mm high into the air and him flying backwards, legs up in the air to form a V. Gar went to fire a shot and the stranger shot his .38 out of his hand. It flew across the basement, sliding across the floor. With him out of the firefight, the shooter advanced in a grimacing Lafayette's direction, stepping over Diablo's sprawled dead body. The shooter's shadow eclipsed Lafayette and he extended his banger downward, right into his mothafucking face, letting off.

Blocka! Blocka! Blocka! Blocka!

"Ol' bitch ass nigga!" he spat on the corpse that he had created and kicked it, causing it to jerk violently. He then casted his eyes on a very shocked Gar, his eyes were still wide open and his mouth ajar.

"Lil…Lil Man, but how are you still alive?"

Blocka! Blocka! Blocka! Lil' Man gave Gar two to the chest and one to the thinking cap, making sure that his days of thugging were over.

"Figure that shit out in hell." The little nigga said, eyebrows arched and nose scrunched up. He lowered his steel and stepped to Victoria. She glared at him. The expression on her face was like, *Go ahead and do it.* She didn't show any fear or submissiveness. Little momma was prepared for whatever was going to happen.

"If you gone kill me now then do it, gone and get the shit over with."

Lil' Man looked her dead in her eyes for what seemed like an eternity. He then pointed his gun at her face. The bitch was a G though, she didn't blink or flinch. Abruptly, he snapped his gun to the side of her face and pulled the trigger. His tool slightly jerked releasing a shot. A spark of fire flew from off of the metal loop on the wall that her chain was shackled to and it clasped to the floor. Lil Man took a deep breath and walked away, leaving the queen pin with furrowed brows. She didn't know why in the hell he had freed her from captivity, but she wasn't about to complain about it. Nah, she was about to get the fuck from up out of there while she still could.

Victoria looked up in time to see Lil' Man disappearing up the staircase. She went about her business to get dressed. The only reason why she stopped was because she heard several barking dogs coming in her direction. Right after, she heard their stampeding feet as they hurried down the steps. All she saw were their hungry eyes and fangs.

The beasts tore into the queen pin and she screamed so loud that her uvula shook at the back of her throat. The canines sunk their teeth into her flesh, sending blood flying everywhere. They tore meat from bone, munching down chunks of her. Through teary eyes, Victoria looked up and saw Lil' Man stepping down on the basement floor.

"I know that nigga La wouldn't have put that check on my head had it not been for you putting the battery in his back, pillow talk is a mothafucka! I knew how my nigga looked at chu, so there was no doubt in my mind that you were behind it!"

"So what? Fuck you! Fuck you!" Tears flooded her face and she managed to throw up the middle finger. As soon as she did, one of the dogs jumped up and bit that mothafucka off. She hollered and fell to the floor. That's when another one of those mean sons of bitches bit down on her neck and ripped her throat out, blood pouring down her chest. She went cock eyed and gagged on her own blood, form rocking back and forth as the dogs devoured her. Lil' Man watched for a time before retreating back up the staircase and through its door, pulling it shut behind him. As he journeyed through the kitchen, he could still hear the beasts feasting on the queen pin down inside of the basement.

Grrrrrrr!

Grrrrrrr!

Grrrrrrr!

Without turning his head, Lil' Man snatched up a dish rag from off of the counter top and wiped off his murder weapon. He dropped it to the floor and continued his stroll through the living room, out of the front door. He came down the steps to a 2016 white convertible drop top Porsche 911. Behind the wheel sat a light skinned nigga with an athletic physique. He was wearing designer shades and a Pistons basketball jersey, chewing gum. He smiled when he saw Lil' Man and opened the door for him. The little nigga slid inside of the sports car and slammed the door shut behind him.

"Is it done, baby?" the man behind the wheel asked.

"Yeah," He nodded.

"All of 'em?"

"Every last one."

"Good. About that gift I got for you." The man behind the wheel reached into the backseat and grabbed a hat box. Smiling, he sat the hat box on Lil' Man's lap. Homie looked from the hat box to the man that had given it to him, wearing a look of wonder on his face, "Gone and open it, baby."

"All right."

"I hope you like it."

"You know my style, I'm sure I will." He removed the lid of the hat box and found Ruby's severed head. Her eyes were bugged and her mouth was stretched wide open. Her face held the mold of him screaming as he was murdered, this was the transgender that was sent to assassinate Lil' Man.

"Thank you, handsome."Lil' Man pulled him closer and kissed him deep and passionately. The man behind the wheel smiled when he pulled away.

"Tell me there's more where that came room."

"When we get home, you're getting the works." Lil' Man promised, caressing his cheek.

"I guess I better put the pedal to the metal." He floored the gas pedal, ripping through the streets. He rode against the wind, jersey ruffling.

"I love you, Jason."

"I love you, too." The attorney replied and they kissed again. Lil' Man laid his head against Jason's shoulder, caressing his arm. He shut his eyelids and a smile stretched across his lips.

"You're a stand-up nigga, baby."

"Oh, yeah? Why do you think that?"

"'Cause you were facing all of that time and didn't snitch. Even when your so called friends turned their backs on you and put that money on your head…you still kept your mouth shut." Jason looked back and forth between Lil' Man and the windshield. "Can't nobody ever say that my man is fake. You're the last last real nigga alive."

The Porsche ripped up the street, being swallowed by the rising orange reddish sun that was slowly creeping upwards into the sky.

EPILOGUE

Ten years later

The C.O. opened the cell's door and Zay came waltzing out, head held high. He moved down the mustard yellow corridor without a care in the world, a quartet of correctional officers and a priest walking along with him.

"Dead man walking! Dead man walking!" The correctional officer closest to him called out.

Zay didn't pay him any mind, though. He just kept right along walking. His knees didn't buckle, his heart didn't beat fast. Hell, he didn't even cry. Nah, homie decided a long time ago that when it was his day to meet death that he was going to do so like a man.

Zay always knew that his lifestyle would lead to death or imprisonment, but he didn't give a mad ass fuck. He couldn't see himself breaking his back for the white man, punching the clock at some 9 to 5 gig. Fuck that. He wanted money; lots and lots of money. And he sure as hell wasn't going to get it working some square job. He did what he did because he wanted to. It wasn't like a nigga had put a gun to his head and made him do it. There were consequences behind his actions, and he knew that someday he'd have to pay for them. It just so happened that today was the day that he was going to have to pay his debt.

The correctional officers led their prisoner to the room where his execution was to take place. The first thing he noticed when he crossed the threshold was the green leather cushioned gurney with all of the straps on it. He knew that he'd be lying upon it when he took his last breath. Homie couldn't help wondering how many niggaz had lay upon that very same gurney to have their life extinguished. Once the chains and shackles were removed from Zay, he was escorted over to the gurney where he was made to lay down. Lying there and staring up at the bright lights in the ceiling, he felt the worn, brown leather straps being pulled and buckled around his wrists, waist and ankles. After the officers made sure that all of the straps were secure, they dispersed so that the doctor performing the procedure could handle the task he was assigned.

The doctor tied a tourniquet around Zay's arm, cleaned it with a swab moistened in alcohol and tapped it until a vein bulged. Once he did this, he put the IV into his arm and removed the length of rubber. He repeated this same routine with the opposite arm, as well. He then opened his patient's shirt and attached the patches that would monitor his heart.

This was done so that the time of his death could be recorded and confirmed.

When the doctor turned around walking off, Zay noticed a machine that housed three large syringes containing three concoctions. He didn't have any idea what the concoctions were called, but he knew that they would assist in his death. At that moment the curtains were being drawn apart from the enormous windows surrounding the diagnostics room, leaving an audience observing him. Among the spectators he found La'Chat. Besides the gray hair she'd grown from stressing and the thirty extra pounds that she'd put on, she looked the same to him. La'Chat's eyes were red webbed and glassy. Her cheeks were wet from all of the tears she'd shed. She kissed the palm of her hand and blew her husband a kiss. Afterwards, she mouthed that she loved him and he mouthed it back.

Zay felt hot sting in his eyes and tears trying to manifest. He batted them away though. He knew that if he cried that those mothafuckaz in the audience would think that he was scared to die. That wasn't the case though. He felt sad because he wouldn't be alive to raise his daughter with his wife. In his death he was leaving them all alone in this God forsaken world. Still, if he could do it all over again, he wouldn't. This was because if he lived any other lifestyle he may have not met La'Chat, fallen madly in love, gotten married and had his first child. If that would have never happened then he believed that he never would have experienced happiness.

The priest approached Zay with the Holy Bible and opened the book. Licking his fingers, he flipped through the pages until he found the one that he was looking for. After reading him a passage, he gave him his blessings and excused himself.

"Any last words?" the warden asked Zay. The room had a PA system, so everyone outside of the glass could hear what he had to say.

"Nah, let's get this shit over with." Zay told him.

And with that, the machinery that housed the syringes was activated and the concoctions were emptied into his veins. Soon after, Zay shut his eyelids and expelled his last breath, leaving this world for the next.

That night

La'Chat lay in bed in her gown, reading over the letter that Zay had written her years ago. The letter was short. Although she had read it one thousand times, she'd never gotten tired of it. In fact, she'd keep it forever. La'Chat got to the end of the letter and read what was left after P.S.

I want you to name our daughter Live. I chose this name because after all that I have been through. After all that I have done to end up in here with this fate, I realize now that life is the most precious thing on this earth. Therefore, I want our

200

beautiful baby girl to live life to the fullest, so when it's all over, she'll have no regrets. Our love will never die, even in my death, Zay and La'Chat forever.

La'Chat snatched the tissues out of the Kleenex box on the nightstand to wipe her tearing eyes and blow her nose. Once she was done, she balled up the tissue and tossed it into the waste basket.

"Forever," she nodded and sniffled. "Always and forever, baby."

THE END

AVAILABLE NOW BY TRANAY ADAMS

The Devil Wears Timbs 1-5

Bury Me A G 1-3

Tyson's Treasure 1-2

Treasure's Pain

A South Central Love Affair

Me And My Hittas 1- 6

The Last Real Nigga Alive 1-3

Fearless

COMING SOON BY TRANAY ADAMS

The Devil Wears Timbs 6: Just Like Daddy

A Hood Nigga's Blues

Billy Bad Ass

9 781732 792258